NORMAN ROCKWELL'S PATRIOTIC TIMES

OTHER NORMAN ROCKWELL BOOKS
BY GEORGE MENDOZA

Norman Rockwell's Americana ABC
Norman Rockwell's Boys and Girls at Play
Norman Rockwell's Diary for a Young Girl
Norman Rockwell's Scrapbook for a Young Boy
Norman Rockwell's Four Seasons
Norman Rockwell's Happy Holidays
Norman Rockwell's Love and Remembrance

NORMAN ROCKWELL'S PATRIOTIC TIMES

George Mendoza

Foreword by Ronald Reagan
President of the United States of America

VIKING

VIKING
Viking Penguin Inc., 40 West 23rd Street,
New York, New York 10010, U.S.A.
Penguin Books Ltd, Harmondsworth,
Middlesex, England
Penguin Books Australia Ltd, Ringwood,
Victoria, Australia
Penguin Books Canada Limited, 2801 John Street,
Markham, Ontario, Canada L3R 1B4
Penguin Books (N.Z.) Ltd, 182–190 Wairau Road,
Auckland 10, New Zealand

Copyright © George Mendoza, 1985
Introduction copyright © Viking Penguin Inc., 1985
All rights reserved

First published in 1985 by Viking Penguin Inc.
Published simultaneously in Canada

Special thanks to Ambassador Jean Gerard;
Fred Fielding, Special Counsel to the President;
Ann Wroblesky, Director, Special Projects for the First Lady;
Elizabeth Penniman of the White House's Speech Writing Office;
Constance Sayre, Vice President, Associate Publisher, Viking;
Nanette Kritzalis, Managing Editor, Viking;
Evelyn deFrees, Executive Assistant, Viking;
and George Sheanshang, attorney and friend.

Book design by Joe Marc Freedman

LIBRARY OF CONGRESS CATALOGING IN PUBLICATION DATA
Mendoza, George.
Norman Rockwell's patriotic times.
1. Rockwell, Norman, 1894–1978. 2. Poetry—
Collections. 3. Quotations, English. I. Rockwell,
Norman, 1894–1978. II. Title.
ND237 .R68M464   1985   759.13   85–8891
ISBN 0-670-80733-8

Pages 205–207 constitute an extension of this copyright page.

Printed in the United States of America
by R. R. Donnelly & Sons Company, Willard, Ohio
Set in Caslon Old Face

Without limiting the rights under copyright reserved above, no part of this publication
may be reproduced, stored in or introduced into a retrieval system, or transmitted, in any
form or by any means (electronic, mechanical, photocopying, recording or otherwise),
without the prior written permission of both the copyright owner and the above publisher
of this book.

This book is
dedicated to the First Lady,
Nancy Reagan,
spirit behind the flag . . .

Sail, sail thy best, ship of Democracy,
Of value is thy freight, 'tis not the Present only,
The Past is also stored in thee,
Thou holdest not the venture of thyself alone,
not of the Western continent alone,
Earth's resume entire floats on thy keel,
O ship, is steadied by thy spars,
With thee Time voyages in trust, the antecedent
nations sink or swim with thee,
With all their ancient struggles, martyrs,
epics, wars, thou bear'st the other continents,
Theirs, theirs as much as thine, the destination-
port triumphant . . .

> Walt Whitman,
> "Thou Mother with Thy Equal Brood,"
> 1872

Norman Rockwell knew as a boy that he wanted nothing so much as to paint. He took his first art lessons at 13, shared a rickety studio with a friend at 16, and, in 1911, at the age of 17, began regular work as an illustrator.

The America in which young Rockwell grew up and launched his career was still mostly a Nation of small towns. Neighbor knew neighbor, farmers visited Main Street to swap tales at the barber shop, and Babe Ruth was just beginning to attract notice as a slugger. In far-off Europe, storm clouds were gathering, but in our country, these were days of sunshine. The American people had tamed a continent, achieved prosperity, and secured peace for our Nation. They were a hard-working, churchgoing people, filled with spirit and faith.

It was this America that Norman Rockwell so deeply loved. For decades, he shared that love with us all.

He produced thousands of paintings and illustrations—over 300 cover illustrations for the *Saturday Evening Post* alone. He pictured old men with round bellies and red cheeks singing Christmas carols; lanky boys plunging into swimming holes; shy young couples lost in the wonderment of new love; and family scenes of contentment and joy—serving the Thanksgiving turkey, tucking the youngsters into bed, and the homecoming of the brave young soldier. Virtually every work strikes a distinctly American note of vibrancy, informality, and humor. The pictures focus not on the rich or mighty, but on everyday Americans and the pleasures of home, outdoors, and family that all of us can enjoy. In this sense, Norman Rockwell's work represents a vivid testimony to the greatness of our democracy.

Our Nation has changed profoundly since the days of the America that Norman Rockwell so skillfully portrayed. Yet the values that he cherished and celebrated—love of God and country, hard work, neighborhood, and family—still give us strength, and will shape our dreams for the decades to come.

I hope you will enjoy as much as Nancy and I have the poems and other patriotic selections assembled here by Mr. Mendoza, along with highlights of Norman Rockwell's illustrations. As we build America's future, we will do well to take inspiration from our Nation's past, and no one captured that past more lovingly than Norman Rockwell, artist and patriot.

NORMAN ROCKWELL'S PATRIOTIC TIMES

I PLEDGE ALLEGIANCE TO THE FLAG OF THE UNITED STATES
OF AMERICA AND TO THE REPUBLIC FOR WHICH IT STANDS,
ONE NATION UNDER GOD, INDIVISIBLE, WITH
LIBERTY AND JUSTICE FOR ALL.

TRIBUTE TO AMERICA

Percy Bysshe Shelley

There is a people mighty in its youth,
    A land beyond the oceans of the west,
Where, though with rudest rites, Freedom and Truth
    Are Worshipt. From a glorious mother's breast,
    Who, since high Athens fell, among the rest
Sate like the Queen of Nations, but in woe,
    By inbred monsters outraged and opprest,
Turns to her chainless child for succor now,
It draws the milk of power in Wisdom's fullest flow.

That land is like an eagle, whose young gaze
    Feeds on the noontide beam, whose golden plume
Floats moveless on the storm, and on the blaze
    Of sunrise gleams when Earth is wrapt in gloom;
    An epitaph of glory for thy tomb
Of murdered Europe may thy fame be made,
Great People! As the sands shalt thou become;
Thy growth is swift as morn when night must fade;
The multitudinous Earth shall sleep beneath thy shade.

Yes, in the desert, there is built a home
    For Freedom! Genius is made strong to rear
The monuments of man beneath the dome
    Of a new Heaven; myriads assemble there
    Whom the proud lords of man, in rage or fear,
Drive from their wasted homes. The boon I pray
    Is this—that Cythna shall be convoyed there,—
Nay, start not at the name—America!

a Family Tree by norman rockwell

WHAT IS AN AMERICAN?

J. Hector St. John de Crèvecoeur

From LETTERS FROM AN AMERICAN FARMER, 1782

What attachment can a poor European emigrant have for a country where he had nothing? The knowledge of the language, the love of a few kindred as poor as himself, were the only cords that tied him. His country is now that which gives him his land, bread, protection, and consequence. . . . What then is the American, this new man? He is neither a European nor the descendant of a European; hence that strange mixture of blood which you will find in no other country. I could point out to you a family whose grandfather was an Englishman, whose wife was Dutch, whose son married a French woman, and whose present four sons have now four wives of different nations. He is an American who, leaving behind him all his ancient prejudices and manners, receives new ones from the new mode of life he has embraced, the new government he obeys, and the new rank he holds. He becomes an American by being received in the broad lap of our great *alma mater.* Here individuals of all nations are melted into a new race of men whose labors and posterity will one day cause great changes in the world. Americans are the western pilgrims, who are carrying along with them the great mass of arts, sciences, vigor, and industry which began long since in the East. They will finish the great circle. The Americans were once scattered all over Europe. Here they are incorporated into one of the finest systems of population which has ever appeared and which will hereafter become distinct by the power of the different climates they inhabit. The American ought therefore to love this country much better than that in which either he or his forefathers were born. Here the rewards of his industry follow with equal steps the progress of his labor. His labor is founded on the basis of nature, *self-interest:* can it want a stronger allurement? Wives and children, who before in vain demanded of him a morsel of bread, now, fat and frolicsome, gladly help their father to clear those fields whence exuberant crops are to rise, to feed and to clothe them all, without any part being claimed either by a despotic prince, a rich abbot, or a mighty lord. Here religion demands but little of him—a small voluntary salary to the minister, and gratitude to God—can he refuse these? The American is a new man who acts on new principles; he must therefore entertain new ideas and form new opinions. From involuntary idleness, servile dependence, penury, and useless labor, he has passed to toils of a very different nature, rewarded by ample subsistence.

This is an American.

THE FOUR FREEDOMS

Norman Rockwell

From NORMAN ROCKWELL:
MY ADVENTURES AS AN
ILLUSTRATOR

But when I left Ben Hibbs' office that day in 1942 after he'd accepted all nine sketches, I was, as I say, still confused. In his shirt sleeves? I thought. The editor of the *Post* in his shirt sleeves? I couldn't understand it. Ben? I thought. Not Mr. Hibbs? I was flummoxed.

Partly, I think, because at the time I couldn't concentrate properly. I was wrestling with a new project and it occupied the better part of my brain. Schaef and I were going to offer our services to the government. Since we were too old to enlist, we had decided that the best way for us to contribute to the war effort was by doing posters for the government. We had already worked up some ideas and were going to set off for Washington any day now. The only thing that was delaying us was me. I hadn't come up with a really good idea yet, one I could get excited about. I had a poster of a machine gunner and a couple of other ideas sketched out, but they didn't satisfy me. I wanted to do something bigger than a war poster, make some statement about why the country was fighting the war.

When Roosevelt and Churchill issued their Atlantic Charter, with its Four Freedoms proclamation, I had tried to read it, thinking that maybe it contained the idea I was looking for. But I hadn't been able to get beyond the first paragraph. The language was so noble, platitudinous really, that it stuck in my throat. No, I said to myself, it doesn't go, how am I to illustrate that? I'm not noble enough. Besides, nobody I know is reading the proclamation either, in spite of the fanfare and hullabaloo about it in the press and on the radio.

So I continued to stew over an idea. I tried this and that. Nothing worked. I juggled the Four Freedoms about in my mind, reading a sentence here, a sentence there, trying to find a picture. But it was so darned high-blown. Somehow I just couldn't get my mind around it.

I did a *Post* cover and an illustration, went to town meeting, attended a Grange supper, struggling all the while with my idea, or rather, the lack of it, what seemed to be a permanent vacuum in my head.

Then one night as I was tossing in bed, mulling over the proclamation and the war, rejecting one idea after another and getting more and more discouraged as the minutes ticked by, all empty and dark, I suddenly remembered how Jim Edgerton had stood up in town meeting and said something that everybody else disagreed with. But they had let him have his say. No one had shouted him down. My gosh, I thought, that's it. There it is. Freedom of

Speech. I'll illustrate the Four Freedoms using my Vermont neighbors as models. I'll express the ideas in simple, everyday scenes. Freedom of Speech —a New England town meeting. Freedom from Want—a Thanksgiving dinner. Take them out of the noble language of the proclamation and put them in terms everybody can understand.

I got all excited. I knew it was the best idea I'd ever had. I ran downstairs to call Schaef. But I couldn't do that; it was three in the morning and I'd disturb all the other people on his party line. So I got my bicycle out of the shed and bicycled over to his house. When I woke him up and told him my idea for the Four Freedoms he got excited too.

In the next couple of days I made rough sketches of the Four Freedoms. Then Schaef and I set off for Washington to offer ourselves to the government.

Orion Wynford, the head of the Creative Department of Brown and Bigelow, a calendar company for whom I did the Boy Scout calendar, met us at the Mayflower Hotel, his white suit and swelling mane of white hair sparkling in the sun. Orion was to take us around to the various government agencies and introduce us to the right people.

We set out the next morning. As we entered the first office the secretary jumped up. "Oh, Mr. Wynford," she said, "thank you so much for the lovely bouquet of roses. And the candy was delicious." Orion smiled and made a deprecatory gesture. At the door of the second office we visited the security guard said, "Swell party, Mr. Wynford. Go right in. *You* don't have to be checked." Evidently Orion had oiled the works.

But, just as evidently, the oil had not penetrated beyond the anterooms. None of the government officials could help us. The war was going badly; nobody had time for posters. Robert Patterson, the Undersecretary of War, said, "We'd love to print your Four Freedoms, but we can't. I'm sorry. We just don't have the time to spare to arrange it. I think they'd be a fine contribution. We'd be delighted if *someone* would publish them."

Schaef and I became more and more discouraged as we were turned down by one official after another. After a while even Orion became rather subdued. Not because our posters weren't being accepted but because his weren't. He was trying to drum up business for Brown and Bigelow. He had a portfolio full of sketches which his company's calendar artists had done. For instance, a beautiful girl leaning forward, bosoms rampant, captioned: *Will you help?*

That was all right. Schaef and I didn't mind if he stropped his own razor while showing us around. But he kept interrupting us. Schaef and I would no more than begin to exhibit our work and explain that we didn't want to be paid for anything, we just wanted to do something for the war effort, than Orion would pull a girly poster from his portfolio and, laying it on the desk in front of the official, say: "Mr. Sec-re-tary. I have here a poster calculated to stir, to

6

inspire, *pride* of country in every American breast. We ask no more than paper to print it on." And he'd continue in this vein, displaying one poster after another, until the Secretary ushered us out of his office, pleading urgent business. So Schaef and I never got to tell our story.

But I doubt whether it would have made any difference. Once Orion excused himself for a minute and we almost jumped on the army colonel in whose office we were at the moment. "We don't want money," we said. "Just let us do our posters." But no, the colonel was sympathetic but helpless; he couldn't arrange it.

Finally, late in the afternoon, we found ourselves in the Office of War Information (or, to speak plainly, the propaganda department). I showed the Four Freedoms to the man in charge of posters but he wasn't even interested. "The last war you illustrators did the posters," he said. "This war we're going to use fine arts men, real artists. If you want to make a contribution to the war effort you can do some of these pen-and-ink drawings for the Marine Corps calisthenics manual. But as far as your Four Freedoms go, we aren't interested." "Well, I don't know," I said, leafing through the layouts of the calisthenics manual (you know, simple drawings of men arms up, arms out, arms to the side), and remembering what high hopes I'd had when I conceived the Four Freedoms, "I guess not." And Schaef, Orion, and I left the office and went back to the hotel. That was the final blow. Schaef and I decided to give up trying to interest people in our posters and my Four Freedoms. The next morning, depressed and discouraged, we took the train back to New York.

But I got off at Philadelphia; I had some sketches to show Ben Hibbs. As I was discussing the sketches with Ben I happened to mention that I'd just been in Washington. "Why?" asked Ben. "Schaef and I were offering our services to the government," I said. "He had some posters and I had a series I wanted to do called the Four Freedoms. No one was interested, though." "Let's see it," said Ben. So I hauled the sketches out and showed them to him, explaining rather listlessly what they were all about, what I'd been trying to do. Ben listened attentively. Then he broke in: "Norman, you've got to do them for us." I could see he was excited. "I'd be delighted to," I said. "Well, drop everything else," said Ben, "just do the Four Freedoms. Don't bother with *Post* covers or illustrations."

So I went back to Arlington, rejuvenated, and set right to work. I spent, finally, six months painting the Four Freedoms and it was a struggle. I had a terrible time. I started the first one I did—"Freedom of Speech"—over four times. I practically finished it twice, finding each time when I had just a few days' work left that it wasn't right. At first I planned to show an entire town meeting, a large hall full of people with one man standing up in the center of the crowd talking. But when I'd got it almost done I found that there were too many people in the picture. It was too diverse, it went every which way and didn't settle anywhere or say anything. So I had to work it over in my mind and, as it turned out, on canvas, until I'd boiled it down into a strong, precise statement: the central figure of the man speaking in the midst of his neighbors.

I wrestled with "Freedom of Worship" for two months. Most of the trouble stemmed from the fact that religion is an extremely delicate subject. It is so easy to hurt so many people's feelings. And the picture was further complicated by my desire to say something about tolerance. I wanted it to make the statement that no man should be discriminated against regardless of his race or religion. My first sketch was of a country barbershop: a Jew in the barber chair, being shaved by a lanky New England barber (obviously a Protestant) while a Catholic priest and a Negro waited their turns. All of them were laughing and getting on well together.

But when I'd just about completed the picture I found that it was no good. The situation bordered on the ridiculous. And the Catholics who came into the studio all said, "Priests don't look like that." (I'd done a stout, rosy-cheeked priest with a bit of a double chin.) And the Negroes thought the Negro's skin should be lighter or darker. And the Jews didn't like my portrayal of the Jew.

So I discarded the picture and started another (I don't remember what it looked like). But that didn't work out either. I started another, junked it. I began to be rather sharp with Jerry and Tom and Peter when they came into the studio to show me a turtle or a frog they'd caught. One day the art editor of the *Post* appeared at the door. Where were the Four Freedoms? "I'm doing them as fast as I can," I snarled politely. Then I wrenched the sketch of the final version of "Freedom of Worship" out of my head and painted it. There is a mystery about the phrase which is lettered across the top of the painting— "Each according to the dictates of his own conscience." I know I read it somewhere but no one has been able to find it in any book or document.

With "Freedom from Want" and "Freedom from Fear" I had little trouble. I painted the turkey in "Freedom from Want" on Thanksgiving Day. Mrs. Wheaton, our cook (and the lady holding the turkey in the picture), cooked it, I painted it, and we ate it. That was one of the few times I've ever eaten the model.

"Freedom from Fear" was based on a rather smug idea. Painted during the bombings of London, it was supposed to say: "Thank God we can put our children to bed with a feeling of security, knowing they will not be killed in the night." I never liked "Freedom from Fear" or, for that matter, "Freedom from Want." Neither of them has any wallop. "Freedom from Want" was not very popular overseas. The Europeans sort of resented it because it wasn't freedom from want, it was overabundance, the table was so loaded down with food. I think the two I had the most trouble with—"Freedom of Speech" and "Freedom of Worship"—have more of an impact, say more, better.

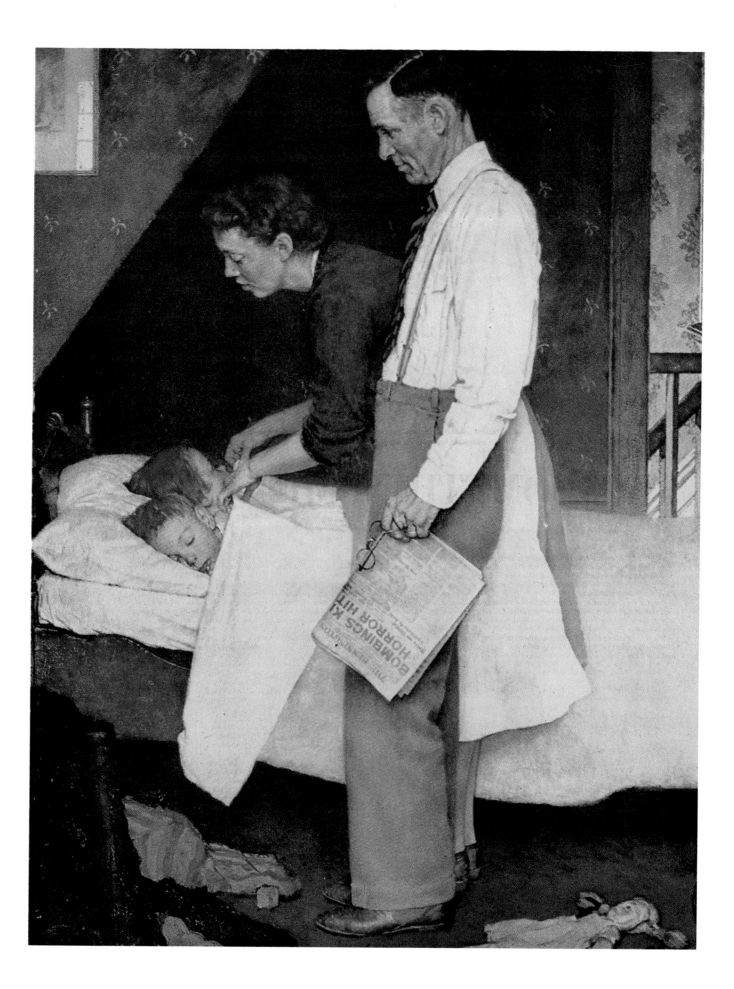

Right about here, with all due immodesty, I'd like to drop in a few paragraphs which Ben Hibbs wrote about the Four Freedoms after reading my account of their inception. "Norman," he said, "I think you ought to say something about what happened after you delivered the Four Freedoms to us." "I can't," I said, "it would sound like boasting." "Well, let me write something," he said. And he did. It delights me. Here it is:

"The result astonished us all," Ben wrote. "The pictures were published early in 1943, not as covers, but as inside features, and each was accompanied by a short essay by some well-known writer saying in words what Rockwell was saying on canvas.

"Requests to reprint flooded in from other publications. Various Government agencies and private organizations made millions of reprints and distributed them not only in this country but all over the world. Those four pictures quickly became the best known and most appreciated paintings of that era. They appeared right at a time when the war was going against us on the battle fronts, and the American people needed the inspirational message which they conveyed so forcefully and so beautifully.

"Subsequently, the Treasury Department took the original paintings on a tour of the nation as the centerpiece of a *Post* art show—to sell war bonds. They were viewed by 1,222,000 people in 16 leading cities and were instrumental in selling $132,992,539 worth of bonds.

"Following the war, the original paintings—they are of heroic size—were hung in our offices. The two which I consider the finest of the four—'Freedom of Worship' and 'Freedom of Speech'—hang in my own office, and I love them. They are a daily source of inspiration to me—in the same way that the clock tower of old Independence Hall, which I can see from my office window, inspires me. If this is Fourth of July talk, so be it. Maybe this country needs a bit more Fourth of July the year around.

"Visitors who come into my office almost always exclaim over the paintings. They marvel at the depth of feeling which Norman was able to build into those pictures. The Four Freedoms originals have been borrowed countless times for art exhibits, and even today we still receive many requests to reprint. However, we have now reached a point where we regard those paintings as so valuable that we rarely permit them to be taken outside the office.

"Many people have asked me whether I regard the 'Freedom of Worship' and the 'Freedom of Speech' as great art. I do. Norman himself probably would disagree. He has always modestly labelled himself an 'illustrator' with no pretensions of fine art. I suspect art critics would say that those two pictures are excellent examples of an illustrator's work at its best, but not great art. I am no art critic, but I still disagree. To me they are great human documents in the form of paint and canvas. A great picture, I think, is one which moves and inspires millions of people. The Four Freedoms did—and do."

To start the war bond drive I went to Washington. At the banquet that night I sat beside a Mrs. Du Pont. She kept trying to bring me out. "Where do you live, Mr. Kent?" she asked (she thought I was Rockwell Kent). "I live in Vermont," I said. "Oh, Thurman," Mrs. Du Pont said, turning to Assistant Attorney General Thurman Arnold who was sitting beside her, "did you hear what Mr. Kent said? The most interesting thing. He said he lives in Vermont." And Mr. Arnold cast a cold, steely, crimebuster eye on Mrs. Du Pont and said nothing. Then Mrs. Du Pont turned back to me: "What is it like in Vermont?" "It's pretty cold," I said. "Thurman," she said, "do you know what Mr. Kent just said?" Again the cold eye: "No." "He said it's quite cold in Vermont." "Ah," Mr. Arnold replied gravely, leaning forward to look at me.

I was flummoxed. I hadn't had a chance to drink a cocktail; I wasn't managing to get anything to eat. Someone was always dragging me off to meet ambassadors or other dignitaries. When the oysters came I was called away for photographs. Just as I sank my fork into the capon some reporters demanded my presence. And now I was being brought out by Mrs. Du Pont. Or rather Rockwell Kent was. In desperation I passed a note to Ben Hibbs: "I'm terrified, and besides, Mrs. Du Pont keeps calling me Rockwell Kent. What'll I do?"

Ben didn't reply and I endured celebrity alone, consoling myself with thoughts of the peaceful green hills and rippling breezes of Vermont.

The next morning, seated on a dais in the midst of a churning sea of people, I autographed reprints of the Four Freedoms at Hecht's Department Store. Women in the crowd were fainting; a lady's petticoat dropped around her ankles as she was standing before me—the place resembled Noah's ark on a hot night.

Late that afternoon I was asked to travel with the Four Freedoms show which was to tour the country, selling bonds. I scratched my head, too worn out to answer. But Ben, God bless him, said, "No, Norman's going to stay home and do *Post* covers." And so the ordeal was over.

NORMAN ROCKWELL'S
AMERICANA ABC

George Mendoza

Who am I?
I am America
as deep and warm,
great and tall,
as Norman Rockwell painted me . . .

A I am an astronaut
on my way to the stars . . .

B I am a boy,
the beginnings of man,
looking out to sea . . .

C I am Christmas and carols
that I wish would stay all year . . .

D I am a dancer
tapping out dreams . . .

E I am the end of the rainbow
where you will find
the land of enchantment . . .

F I am a family tree.
Do you know where
you came from . . . ?

G I am the Golden Rule,
a good idea to think about . . .

H I am a heart of love
that means
you're mine forever . . .

I I am an ice-skater
with a young boy's way . . .

J I am a jester,
a clown
sometimes happy
and sometimes sad . . .

K I am a kite-flyer
fishing for clouds . . .

L I am the land as far as I can see,
before and after me . . .

M I am a mirror filled with
the magic of tomorrow . . .

N I am your new neighbor
and soon we will play together . . .

O I am old MacDonald
who had a farm,
E-I-E-I-O . . .

P I am all the prayers in you . . .

Q I am the quiet time of each falling night . . .

R I am a riverboat race
up the Connecticut
coming hard . . .

S I am the seasons of the year,
a revolving door
for all the things you like to do . . .

T I am the turkey on your table
and the joy of giving thanks . . .

U I am Uncle Sam
and I am going to fly
with you forever . . .

V I am vacation time,
eager for it,
Or glad it's over . . .

W I'm the wings of an eagle soaring gold . . .

X I am the X that marks the spot . . .

Y I am Yankee Doodle came to town
Riding on a pony
Stuck a feather in his hat
And called it macaroni . . .

Z I am "Zip-a-dee doo-dah,
Zip-a-dee ay,
my, oh my, what a wonderful day . . ."

I am America.
I begin with A
and I end in a.
I am America
as long ago as I can remember
and as far ahead as I can dream.

STARTING FROM PAUMANOK

Walt Whitman

1

Starting from fish-shape Paumanok where I was born,
Well-begotten, and rais'd by a perfect mother,
After roaming many lands, lover of populous pavements,
Dweller in Mannahatta my city, or on southern savannas,
Or a soldier camp'd or carrying my knapsack and gun, or a miner in California,
Or rude in my home in Dakota's woods, my diet meat, my drink from the spring,
Or withdrawn to muse and meditate in some deep recess,
Far from the clank of crowds intervals passing rapt and happy,
Aware of the fresh free giver the flowing Missouri, aware of mighty Niagara,
Aware of the buffalo herds grazing the plains, the hirsute and strong-breasted bull,
Of earth, rocks, Fifth-month flowers experienced, stars, rain, snow, my amaze,
Having studied the mocking-bird's tones and the flight of the mountainhawk,
And heard at dawn the unrivall'd one, the hermit thrush from the swamp-cedars,
Solitary, singing in the West, I strike up for a New World.

2

Victory, union, faith, identity, time,
The indissoluble compacts, riches, mystery,
Eternal progress, the kosmos, and the modern reports.

This then is life,
Here is what has come to the surface after so many throes and convulsions.

How curious! how real!
Underfoot the divine soil, overhead the sun.

See revolving the globe,
The ancestor-continents away group'd together,
The present and future continents north and south, with the isthmus between.

See, vast trackless spaces,
As in a dream they change, they swiftly fill,
Countless masses debouch upon them,
They are now cover'd with the foremost people, arts, institutions, known.

See, projected through time,
For me an audience interminable.

With firm and regular step they wend, they never stop,
Successions of men, Americanos, a hundred millions,
One generation playing its part and passing on,
Another generation playing its part and passing on in its turn,
With faces turn'd sideways or backward towards me to listen,
With eyes retrospective towards me.

3

Americanos! conquerors! marches humanitarian!
Foremost! century marches! Libertad! masses!
For you a programme of chants.

Chants of the prairies,
Chants of the long-running Mississippi, and down to the Mexican sea,
Chants of Ohio, Indiana, Illinois, Iowa, Wisconsin and Minnesota,
Chants going forth from the centre from Kansas, and thence equidistant,
Shooting in pulses of fire ceaseless to vivify all.

4

Take my leaves America, take them South and take them North,
Make welcome for them everywhere, for they are your own offspring,
Surround them East and West, for they would surround you,
And you precedents, connect lovingly with them, for they connect lovingly with you.

I conn'd old times,
I sat studying at the feet of the great masters,
Now if eligible O that the great masters might return and study me.

In the name of these States shall I scorn the antique?
Why these are the children of the antique to justify it.

5

Dead poets, philosophs, priests,
Martyrs, artists, inventors, governments long since,
Language-shapers on other shores,
Nations once powerful, now reduced, withdrawn, or desolate,

I dare not proceed till I respectfully credit what you have left wafted hither,
I have perused it, own it is admirable (moving awhile among it),
Think nothing can ever be greater, nothing can ever deserve more than it deserves,
Regarding it all intently a long while, then dismissing it,
I stand in my place with my own day here.

Here lands female and male,
Here the heir-ship and heiress-ship of the world, here the flame of materials,
Here spirituality the translatress, the openly-avow'd,
The ever-tending, the finalè of visible forms,
The satisfier, after due long-waiting now advancing,
Yes here comes my mistress the soul.

6

The soul,
Forever and forever—longer than soil is brown and solid—longer than water ebbs and flows.

I will make the poems of materials, for I think they are to be the most spiritual poems,
And I will make the poems of my body and of mortality,
For I think I shall then supply myself with the poems of my soul and of immortality.

I will make a song for these States that no one State may under any circumstances be subjected to another
    State,
And I will make a song that there shall be comity by day and by night between all the States, and between any
    two of them,
And I will make a song for the ears of the President, full of weapons with menacing points,
And behind the weapons countless dissatisfied faces;
And a song make I of the One form'd out of all,
The fang'd and glittering One whose head is over all,
Resolute warlike One including and over all,
(However high the head of any else that head is over all.)
I will acknowledge contemporary lands,
I will trail the whole geography of the globe and salute courteously every city large and small,
And employments! I will put in my poems that with you is heroism upon land and sea,
And I will report all heroism from an American point of view.

I will sing the song of companionship,
I will show what alone must finally compact these,
I believe these are to found their own ideal of manly love, indicating it in me,
I will therefore let flame from me the burning fires that were threatening to consume me,
I will lift what has too long kept down those smouldering fires,

I will give them complete abandonment,
I will write the evangel-poem of comrades and of love,
For who but I should understand love with all its sorrow and joy?
And who but I should be the poet of comrades?

7

I am the credulous man of qualities, ages, races,
I advance from the people in their own spirit,
Here is what sings unrestricted faith.

Omnes! omnes! let others ignore what they may,
I make the poem of evil also, I commemorate that part also,
I am myself just as much evil as good, and my nation is—and I say there is in fact no evil,
(Or if there is I say it is just as important to you, to the land or to me, as anything else.)

I too, following many and follow'd by many, inaugurate a religion, I descend into the arena,
(It may be I am destin'd to utter the loudest cries there, the winner's pealing shouts,
Who knows? they may rise from me yet, and soar above everything.)

Each is not for its own sake,
I say the whole earth and all the stars in the sky are for religion's sake.

I say no man has ever yet been half devout enough,
None has ever yet adored or worship'd half enough,
None has begun to think how divine he himself is, and how certain the future is.

I say that the real and permanent grandeur of these States must be their religion,
Otherwise there is no real and permanent grandeur;
(Nor character nor life worthy the name without religion,
Nor land nor man or woman without religion.)

8

What are you doing young man?
Are you so earnest, so given up to literature, science, art, amours?
These ostensible realities, politics, points?
Your ambition or business whatever it may be?

It is well—against such I say not a word, I am their poet also,
But behold! such swiftly subside, burnt up for religion's sake,
For not all matter is fuel to heat, impalpable flame, the essential life of the earth,
Any more than such are to religion.

9

What do you seek so pensive and silent?
What do you need camerado?
Dear son do you think it is love?

Listen dear son—listen America, daughter or son,
It is a painful thing to love a man or woman to excess, and yet it satisfies, it is great,
But there is something else very great, it makes the whole coincide,
It, magnificent, beyond materials, with continuous hands sweeps and provides for all.

10

Know you, solely to drop in the earth the germs of a greater religion,
The following chants each for its kind I sing.

My comrade!
For you to share with me two greatnesses, and a third one rising inclusive and more resplendent,
The greatness of Love and Democracy, and the greatness of Religion.
Melange mine own, the unseen and the seen,
Mysterious ocean where the streams empty,
Prophetic spirit of materials shifting and flickering around me,
Living beings, identities now doubtless near us in the air that we know not of,
Contact daily and hourly that will not release me,
These selecting, these in hints demanded of me.

Not he with a daily kiss onward from childhood kissing me,
Has winded and twisted around me that which holds me to him,
Any more than I am held to the heavens and all the spiritual world,
After what they have done to me, suggesting themes.

O such themes—equalities! O divine average!
Warblings under the sun, usher'd as now, or at noon, or setting,
Strains musical flowing through ages, now reaching hither,
I take to your reckless and composite chords, add to them, and cheerfully pass them forward.

11

As I have walk'd in Alabama my morning walk,
I have seen where the she-bird the mocking-bird sat on her nest in the briers hatching her brood.

I have seen the he-bird also,
I have paus'd to hear him near at hand inflating his throat and joyfully singing.

And while I paus'd it came to me that what he really sang for was not there only,
Nor for his mate nor himself only, nor all sent back by the echoes,
But subtle, clandestine, away beyond,
A charge transmitted and gift occult for those being born.

12

Democracy! near at hand to you a throat is now inflating itself and joyfully singing.

Ma femme! for the brood beyond us and of us,
For those who belong here and those to come,
I exultant to be ready for them will now shake out carols stronger and haughtier than have ever yet been heard
    upon earth.

I will make the songs of passion to give them their way,
And your songs outlaw'd offenders, for I scan you with kindred eyes, and carry you with me the same as any.

I will make the true poem of riches,
To earn for the body and the mind whatever adheres and goes forward and is not dropt by death;
I will effuse egotism and show it underlying all, and I will be the bard of personality,
And I will show of male and female that either is but the equal of the other,
And sexual organs and acts! do you concentrate in me, for I am determin'd to tell you with courageous clear
    voice to prove you illustrious,
And I will show that there is no imperfection in the present, and can be none in the future,
And I will show that whatever happens to anybody it may be turn'd to beautiful results,
And I will show that nothing can happen more beautiful than death,
And I will thread a thread through my poems that time and events are compact,
And that all the things of the universe are perfect miracles, each as profound as any.

I will not make poems with reference to parts,
But I will make poems, songs, thoughts, with reference to ensemble,
And I will not sing with reference to a day, but with reference to all days,
And I will not make a poem nor the least part of a poem but has reference to the soul,
Because having look'd at the objects of the universe, I find there is no one nor any particle of one but has
    reference to the soul.

13

Was somebody asking to see the soul?
See, your own shape and countenance, persons, substances, beasts, the trees, the running rivers, the rocks and
    sands.

All hold spiritual joys and afterwards loosen them;
How can the real body ever die and be buried?
Of your real body and any man's or woman's real body,
Item for item it will elude the hands of the corpse-cleaners and pass to fitting spheres,
Carrying what has accrued to it from the moment of birth to the moment of death.

Not the types set up by the printer return their impression, the meaning, the main concern,
Any more than a man's substance and life or a woman's substance and life return in the body and the soul,
Indifferently before death and after death.

Behold, the body includes and is the meaning, the main concern, and includes and is the soul;
Whoever you are, how superb and how divine is your body, or any part of it!

14

Whoever you are, to you endless announcements!

Daughter of the lands did you wait for your poet?
Did you wait for one with a flowing mouth and indicative hand?

Toward the male of the States, and toward the female of the States,
Exulting words, words to Democracy's lands.

Interlink'd, food-yielding lands!
Land of coal and iron! land of gold! land of cotton, sugar, rice!
Land of wheat, beef, pork! land of wool and hemp! land of the apple and the grape!
Land of the pastoral plains, the grass-fields of the world! land of those sweet-air'd interminable plateaus!
Land of the herd, the garden, the healthy house of adobie!
Lands where the north-west Columbia winds, and where the south-west Colorado winds!
Land of the eastern Chesapeake! land of the Delaware!
Land of Ontario, Erie, Huron, Michigan!
Land of the Old Thirteen! Massachusetts land! land of Vermont and Connecticut!
Land of the ocean shores! land of sierras and peaks!
Land of boatmen and sailors! fishermen's land!
Inextricable lands! the clutch'd together! the passionate ones!
The side by side! the elder and younger brothers! the bony-limb'd!
The great women's land! the feminine! the experienced sisters and the inexperienced sisters!
For breath'd land! Arctic braced! Mexican breez'd! the diverse! the compact!
The Pennsylvanian! the Virginian! the double Carolinian!
O all and each well-loved by me! my intrepid nations! O I at any rate include you all with perfect love!
I cannot be discharged from you! not from one any sooner than another!

O death, O for all that, I am yet of you unseen this hour with irrepressible love,
Walking New England, a friend, a traveler,
Splashing my bare feet in the edge of the summer ripples on Paumanok's sands,
Crossing the prairies, dwelling again in Chicago, dwelling in every town,
Observing shows, births, improvements, structures, arts,
Listening to orators and oratresses in public halls,
Of and through the States as during life, each man and woman my neighbor,
The Louisianian, the Georgian, as near to me, and I as near to him and her,
The Mississippian and Arkansian yet with me, and I yet with any of them,
Yet upon the plains west of the spinal river, yet in my house of adobe,
Yet returning eastward, yet in the Seaside State or in Maryland,
Yet Kanadian cheerily braving the winter, the snow and ice welcome to me,
Yet a true son either of Maine or of the Granite State, or the Narragansett Bay State, or the Empire State,
Yet sailing to other shores to annex the same, yet welcoming every new brother,
Hereby applying these leaves to the new ones from the hour they unite with the old ones,
Coming among the new ones myself to be their companion and equal, coming personally to you now,
Enjoining you to acts, characters, spectacles, with me.

15

With me with firm holding, yet haste, haste on.

For your life adhere to me,
(I may have to be persuaded many times before I consent to give myself really to you, but what of that?
Must not Nature be persuaded many times?)
No dainty dolce affettuoso I,
Bearded, sun-burnt, gray-neck'd, forbidding, I have arrived,
To be wrestled with as I pass for the solid prizes of the universe,
For such I afford whoever can persevere to win them.

16

On my way a moment I pause,
Here for you! and here for America!
Still the present I raise aloft, still the future of the States I harbinge glad and sublime,
And for the past I pronounce what the air holds of the red aborigines.

The red aborigines,
Leaving natural breaths, sounds of rain and winds, calls as of birds and animals in the woods, syllabled to us
    for names,
Okonee, Koosa, Ottawa, Monnogahela, Sauk, Natchez, Chattahoochee, Kaqueta, Oronoco,
Wabash, Miami, Saginaw, Chippewa, Oshkosh, Walla-Walla,
Leaving such to the States they melt, they depart, charging the water and the land with names.

17

Expanding and swift, henceforth,
Elements, breeds, adjustments, turbulent, quick and audacious,
A world primal again, vistas of glory incessant and branching,
A new race dominating previous ones and grander far, with new contests,
New politics, new literatures and religions, new inventions and arts.

These, my voice announcing—I will sleep no more but arise,
You oceans that have been calm within me! how I feel you, fathomless, stirring, preparing unprecedented
    waves and storms.

18

See, steamers steaming through my poems,
See, in my poems immigrants continually coming and landing,
See, in arriere, the wigwam, the trail, the hunter's hut, the flat-boat, the maize-leaf, the claim, the rude
    fence, and the backwoods village,
See, on the one side the Western Sea and on the other the Eastern Sea, how they advance and retreat upon my
    poems as upon their own shores,
See, pastures and forests in my poems—see, animals wild and tame—see, beyond the Kaw, countless herds of
    buffalo feeding on short curly grass,
See, in my poems, cities, solid, vast, inland, with paved streets, with iron and stone edifices, ceaseless
    vehicles, and commerce,
See, the many-cylinder'd steam printing-press—see, the electric telegraph stretching across the continent,
See, through Atlantica's depths pulses American Europe reaching, pulses of Europe duly return'd,
See, the strong and quick locomotive as it departs, panting, blowing the steam-whistle,
See, ploughmen ploughing farms—see, miners digging mines—see, the numberless factories,
See, mechanics busy at their benches with tools—see from among them superior judges, philosophs, Presi-
    dents, emerge, drest in working dresses,
See, lounging through the shops and fields of the States, me well-belov'd, close-held by day and night,
Hear the loud echoes of my songs here—read the hints come at last.

19

O camerado close! O you and me at last, and us two only.
O a word to clear one's path ahead endlessly!
O something ecstatic and undemonstrable! O music wild!
O now I triumph—and you shall also;
O hand in hand—O wholesome pleasure—O one more desirer and lover!
O to haste firm holding—to haste, haste on with me.

THE PEOPLE WILL LIVE ON

Carl Sandburg

The people will live on.
The learning and blundering people will live on.
They will be tricked and sold and again sold
And go back to the nourishing earth for rootholds,
The people so peculiar in renewal and comeback,
You can't laugh off their capacity to take it.
The mammoth rests between his cyclonic dramas.

The people so often sleepy, weary, enigmatic,
is a vast huddle with many units saying:
"I earn my living
I make enough to get by
and it takes all my time.
If I had more time
I could do more for myself
and maybe for others.
I could ready and study
and talk things over
and find out about things.
It takes time.
I wish I had the time."

The people is a tragic and comic two-face:
hero and hoodlum: phantom and gorilla twist-
ing to moan with a gargoyle mouth: "They
buy me and sell me . . . it's a game . . .
sometimes I'll break loose . . ."

Once having marched
Over the margins of animal necessity,
Over the grim line of sheer subsistence
Then man came
To the deeper rituals of his bones,
To the lights lighter than any bones,
To the time for thinking things over,
To the dance, the song, the story,
Or the hours given over to dreaming,
Once having so marched.

Between the finite limitations of the five senses
and the endless yearnings of man for the beyond
the people hold to the humdrum bidding of work and food
while reaching out when it comes their way
for lights beyond the prison of the five senses,
for keepsakes lasting beyond any hunger or death.
      This reaching is alive.
The panderers and liars have violated and smutted it.
      Yet this reaching is alive yet
      for lights and keepsakes.

      The people know the salt of the sea
      and the strength of the winds
      lashing the corners of the earth.
      The people take the earth
      as a tomb of rest and a cradle of hope.
      Who else speaks for the Family of Man?
      They are in tune and step
      with constellations of universal law.

      The people is a polychrome,
      a spectrum and a prism
      held in a moving monolith,
      a console organ of changing themes,
      a clavilux of color poems
      wherein the sea offers fog
      and the fog moves off in rain
      and the Labrador sunset shortens
      to a nocturne of clear stars
      serene over the shot spray
      of northern lights.

      The steel mill sky is alive.
      The fire breaks white and zigzag
      shot on a gun-metal gloaming.
      Man is a long time coming.
      Man will yet win.
      Brother may yet line up with brother:

This old anvil laughs at many broken hammers.
      There are men who can't be bought.
      The fireborn are at home in fire.
      The stars make no noise.

You can't hinder the wind from blowing.
Time is a great teacher.
Who can live without hope?

In the darkness with a great bundle of grief
    the people march.
In the night, and overhead a shovel of stats for
    keeps, the people march: "Where to? What next?"

From THE BRIDGE

Hart Crane

From going to and fro in the earth,
and from walking up and down in it.
—The Book of Job

PROEM: TO BROOKLYN BRIDGE

How many dawns, chill from his rippling rest
The seagull's wings shall dip and pivot him,
Shedding white rings of tumult, building high
Over the chained bay waters Liberty—

Then, with inviolate curve, forsake our eyes
As apparitional as sails that cross
Some page of figures to be filed away;
—Till elevators drop us from our day. . . .

I think of cinemas, panoramic sleights
With multitudes bent toward some flashing scene
Never disclosed, but hastened to again,
Foretold to other eyes on the same screen;

And Thee, across the harbor, silver-paced
As though the sun took step of thee, yet left
Some motion ever unspent in thy stride,—
Implicitly thy freedom staying thee!

Out of some subway scuttle, cell or loft
A bedlamite speeds to thy parapets,
Tilting there momently, shrill shirt ballooning,
A jest falls from the speechless caravan.

Down Wall, from girder into street noon leaks,
A rip-tooth of the sky's acetylene;
All afternoon the cloud-flown derricks turn. . . .
They cables breathe the North Atlantic still.

And obscure as that heaven of the Jews,
Thy guerdon. . . . Accolade thou dost bestow
Of anonymity time cannot raise:
Vibrant reprieve and pardon thou dost show.

O harp and altar, of the fury fused,
(How could mere toil align thy choiring strings!)
Terrific threshold of the prophet's pledge,
Prayer of pariah, and the lover's cry,—

Again the traffic lights that skim thy swift
Unfractioned idiom, immaculate sigh of stars,
Beading thy path—condense eternity:
And we have seen night lifted in thine arms.

Under thy shadow by the piers I waited;
Only in darkness is thy shadow clear.
The City's fiery parcels all undone,
Already snow submerges an iron year. . . .

O Sleepless as the river under thee,
Vaulting the sea, the prairies' dreaming sod,
Unto us lowliest sometimes sweep, descend
And of the curveship lend a myth to God.

INAUGURAL ADDRESS

John F. Kennedy

We observe today not a victory of party but a celebration of freedom—symbolizing an end as well as a beginning—signifying renewal as well as change. For I have sworn before you and Almighty God the same solemn oath our forebears prescribed nearly a century and three-quarters ago.

The world is very different now. For man holds in his mortal hands the power to abolish all forms of human poverty and all forms of human life. And yet the same revolutionary beliefs for which our forebears fought are still at issue around the globe—the belief that the rights of man come not from the generosity of the state but from the hand of God.

We dare not forget today that we are the heirs of that first revolution. Let the word go forth from this time and place, to friend and foe alike, that the torch has been passed to a new generation of Americans—born in this century, tempered by war, disciplined by a hard and bitter peace, proud of our ancient heritage—and unwilling to witness or permit the slow undoing of those human rights to which this nation has always been committed, and to which we are committed today at home and around the world.

Let every nation know, whether it wishes us well or ill, that we shall pay any price, bear any burden, meet any hardship, support any friend, oppose any foe to assure the survival and the success of liberty.

This much we pledge—and more.

To those old allies whose cultural and spiritual origins we share, we pledge the loyalty of faithful friends. United, there is little we cannot do in a host of cooperative ventures. Divided, there is little we can do—for we dare not meet a powerful challenge at odds and split asunder.

To those new states whom we welcome to the ranks of the free, we pledge our word that one form of colonial control shall not have passed away merely to be replaced by a far more iron tyranny. We shall not always expect to find them supporting our view. But we shall always hope to find them strongly supporting their own freedom—and to remember that, in the past, those who foolishly sought power by riding the back of the tiger ended up inside.

To those people in the huts and villages of half the globe struggling to break the bonds of mass misery, we pledge our best efforts to help them help themselves, for whatever period is required—not because the Communists may be doing it, not because we seek their votes, but because it is right. If a free society cannot help the many who are poor, it cannot save the few who are rich.

To our sister republics south of our border, we offer a special pledge—to convert our good words into good deeds—in a new alliance for progress—to assist free men and free governments in casting off the chains of poverty. But this peaceful revolution of hope cannot become the prey of hostile powers. Let all our neighbors know that we shall join with them to oppose aggression or subversion anywhere in the Americas. And let every other power know that this hemisphere intends to remain the master of its own house.

To that world assembly of sovereign states, the United Nations, our last best hope in an age where the instruments of war have far outpaced the instruments of peace, we renew our pledge of support—to prevent it from becoming merely a forum for invective—to strengthen its shield of the new and the weak—and to enlarge the area in which its writ may run.

Finally, to those nations who would make themselves our adversary, we offer not a pledge but a request—that both sides begin anew the quest for peace before the dark powers of destruction unleashed by science engulf all humanity in planned or accidental self-destruction. We dare not tempt them with weakness. For only when our arms are sufficient beyond doubt can we be certain beyond doubt that they will never be employed.

But neither can two great and powerful groups of nations take comfort from our present course—both sides overburdened by the cost of modern weapons, both rightly alarmed by the steady spread of the deadly atom, yet both racing to alter that uncertain balance of terror that stays the hand of mankind's final war.

So let us begin anew—remembering on both sides that civility is not a sign of weakness, and sincerity is always subject to proof. Let us never negotiate out of fear. But let us never fear to negotiate.

Let both sides explore what problems unite us instead of belaboring those problems which divide us.

Let both sides, for the first time, formulate serious and precise proposals for the inspection and control of arms—and bring the absolute power to destroy other nations under the absolute control of all nations.

Let both sides seek to invoke the wonders of science instead of its terrors. Together let us explore the stars, conquer the deserts, eradicate disease, tap the ocean depths, and encourage the arts and commerce.

Let both sides unite to heed in all corners of the earth the command of Isaiah—to "undo the heavy burdens . . . [and] let the oppressed go free."

And if a beachhead of cooperation may push back the jungle of suspicion, let both sides join in creating a new endeavor, not a new balance of power but a new world of law, where the strong are just and the weak secure and the peace preserved.

All this will not be finished in the first 100 days. Nor will it be finished in the first 1,000 days, nor in the life of this administration, nor even perhaps in our lifetime on this planet. But let us begin.

In your hands, my fellow citizens, more than mine, will rest the final success or failure of our course. Since this country was founded, each generation of Americans has been summoned to give testimony to its national loyalty. The graves of young Americans who answered the call to service surround the globe.

Now the trumpet summons us again—not as a call to bear arms, though arms we need—not as a call to battle, though embattled we are—but a call to bear the burden of a long twilight struggle, year in and year out, "rejoicing in hope, patient in tribulation"—a struggle against the common enemies of man: tyranny, poverty, disease, and war itself.

Can we forge against these enemies a grand and global alliance, North and South, East and West, that can assure a more fruitful life for all mankind? Will you join in that historic effort?

In the long history of the world, only a few generations have been granted the role of defending freedom in its hour of maximum danger. I do not shrink from this responsibility—I welcome it. I do not believe that any of us would exchange places with any other people or any other generation. The energy, the faith, the devotion which we bring to this endeavor will light our country and all who serve it—and the glow from that fire can truly light the world.

And so, my fellow Americans—ask not what your country can do for you—ask what you can do for your country.

My fellow citizens of the world—ask not what America will do for you but what together we can do for the freedom of man.

Finally, whether you are citizens of America or citizens of the world, ask of us here the same high standards of strength and sacrifice which we ask of you. With a good conscience our only sure reward, with history the final judge of our deeds, let us go forth to lead the land we love, asking His blessing and His help, but knowing that here on earth God's work must truly be our own.

THE GIFT OUTRIGHT

Robert Frost

The land was ours before we were the land's.
She was our land more than a hundred years
Before we were her people. She was ours
In Massachusetts, in Virginia,
But we were England's, still colonials,
Possessing what we still were unpossessed by,
Possessed by what we now no more possessed.
Something we were withholding left us weak
Until we found out that it was ourselves
We were withholding from our land of living
And forthwith found salvation in surrender.
Such as we were we gave ourselves outright
(The deed of gift was many deeds of war)
To the land vaguely realizing westward,
But still unstoried, artless, unenhanced,
Such as she was, such as she would become.

From THE STORY OF THE UNITED STATES FLAG

Wyatt Blassingame

5. "AND THE ROCKET'S RED GLARE . . ."

During the early days of the United States there was not much interest in the national flag. Because the nation was new, many people felt more loyal to their home state than to the nation. The state flags seemed more important than the Stars and Stripes. Then in 1812 the United States went to war with England for the second time. During this war something happened that made people deeply conscious and proud of their national flag.

The War of 1812 did not start well for the United States. British troops captured Washington, D.C., the nation's capital. Here they arrested an American doctor named William Beanes. He was taken to one of the British warships in Chesapeake Bay.

Dr. Beanes had a friend named Francis Scott Key, a lawyer who liked to write poetry. When Key heard of Beanes' arrest, he went in a small boat to the ship where Beanes was held. He asked the British admiral to set Dr. Beanes free.

Finally the Admiral agreed. "However," he said, "I cannot let either you or Dr. Beanes go ashore now. We are going to attack Baltimore. I will have to hold you prisoner until the fight is over."

The British fleet sailed up the Bay. At daylight on September 13, 1814, it lay in the harbor outside Baltimore, Maryland. Between the fleet and the city was Fort McHenry. Over the fort waved an American flag.

It was a huge flag, 42 feet long and 30 feet wide, with fifteen red and white stripes. From the deck of the British ship, Key watched the great flag ripple in the morning breeze. His heart beat proudly at the sight.

One of the British ships flashed a signal. An instant later the guns of the fleet began to roar. The ship on which Key was held prisoner did not join in the fighting. But from it Key could see the British shells striking the fort. He could see the flash of the American guns in return.

A shell tore through the huge flag. Flying splinters ripped it. But still the flag waved in the wind. Key knew that, as long as the flag was there, the fort was in American hands.

The battle went on all day and into the night. By the flash of the exploding shells, Key could see the flag.

Sometime during the night it began to rain. Key could no longer see the flag, or tell how the battle was going. But still he stood in the rain, watching and listening.

Toward dawn the rain stopped. The firing stopped too. The battle was over, but who had won?

Daylight came slowly. Fog lay low over the water. Sometimes, when the fog parted, Key could see the fort. There was a flag—but he could not tell what flag. Then a slanting beam of sunlight touched on the banner, and the colors glowed in the light.

It was the Stars and Stripes! The British ships were turning away. The Americans had won!

Deeply moved by what he had seen, Francis Scott Key wrote a poem. He did not name it, but it was soon called "The Star-Spangled Banner."

> *O! say, can you see by the dawn's*
>   *early light,*
> *What so proudly we hailed at the twilight's last gleaming:*
> *Whose broad stripes and bright stars,*
>   *through the perilous fight,*
> *O'er the ramparts we watched were so*
>   *gallantly streaming,*
> *And the rocket's red glare, the bombs*
>   *bursting in air,*
> *Gave proof through the night that*
>   *our flag was still there;*
> *O! say, does the Star-Spangled Banner yet wave*
> *O'er the land of the free and the*
>   *home of the brave?*

Set to an old popular tune, "The Star-Spangled Banner" was soon being sung all over the country. Today it is the official National Anthem of the United States.

OUR INTELLECTUAL DECLARATION OF INDEPENDENCE

Ralph Waldo Emerson

Thus far, our holiday has been simply a friendly sign of the survival of the love of letters amongst a people too busy to give to letters any more. As such it is precious as the sign of an indestructible instinct. Perhaps the time is already come when it ought to be, and will be, something else; when the sluggard intellect of this continent will look from under its iron lids and fill the postponed expectation of the world with something better than the exertions of mechanical skill. Our day of dependence, our long apprenticeship to the learning of other lands, draws to a close. The millions that around us are rushing into life, cannot always be fed on the sere remains of foreign harvests. Events, actions arise, that must be sung, that will sing themselves. Who can doubt that poetry will revive and lead in a new age, as the star in the constellation Harp, which now flames in our zenith, astronomers announce, shall one day be the pole-star for a thousand years?

SESQUI·CENTENNIAL·CELEBRATION
OF·THE·SIGNING·OF·THE
DECLARATION·OF·INDEPENDENCE

GOD, GIVE US MEN!

Josiah Gilbert Holland

God, give us men! A time like this demands
Strong minds, great hearts, true faith and ready hands;
   Men whom the lust of office does not kill;
Men whom the spoils of office cannot buy;
   Men who possess opinions and a will;
Men who have honor; men who will not lie;
Men who can stand before a demagogue
   And damn his treacherous flatteries without winking!
Tall men, sun-crowned, who live above the fog
   In public duty and in private thinking;
For while the rabble, with their thumb-worn creeds,
Their large professions and their little deeds,
Mingle in selfish strife, lo! Freedom weeps,
Wrong rules the land and waiting Justice sleeps.

A MESSAGE TO GARCIA

Elbert Hubbard

In all this Cuban business there is one man stands out on the horizon of my memory like Mars at perihelion.

When war broke out between Spain and the United States, it was very necessary to communicate quickly with the leader of the Insurgents. Garcia was somewhere in the mountain fastnesses of Cuba—no one knew where. No mail or telegraph message could reach him. The President must secure his co-operation, and quickly.

What to do!

Someone said to the President, "There is a fellow by the name of Rowan who will find Garcia for you, if anybody can."

Rowan was sent for and given a letter to be delivered to Garcia. How the "fellow by the name of Rowan" took the letter, sealed it up in an oilskin pouch, strapped it over his heart, in four days landed by night off the coast of Cuba from an open boat, disappeared into the jungle, and in three weeks came out on the other side of the Island, having traversed a hostile country on foot and delivered his letter to Garcia—are things I have no special desire now to tell in detail. The point that I wish to make is this: McKinley gave Rowan a letter to be delivered to Garcia; Rowan took the letter and did not ask, "Where is he at?"

By the Eternal! there is a man whose form should be cast in deathless bronze and the statue placed in every college of the land. It is not book-learning young men need, nor instruction about this and that, but a stiffening of the vertebrae which will cause them to be loyal to a trust, to act promptly, concentrate their energies: do the thing—"Carry a message to Garcia."

General Garcia is dead now, but there are other Garcias. No man who has endeavored to carry out an enterprise where many hands were needed, but has been well-nigh appalled at times by the imbecility of the average man—the inability or unwillingness to concentrate on a thing and do it.

Slipshod assistance, foolish inattention, dowdy indifference, and half-hearted work seem the rule; and no man succeeds, unless by hook or crook or threat he forces or bribes other men to assist him; or mayhap, God in His goodness performs a miracle, and sends him an Angel of Light for an assistant.

You, reader, put this matter to a test: You are sitting now in your office—six clerks are within call. Summon any one and make this request: "Please look in the encyclopedia and make a brief memorandum for me concerning the life of Correggio."

Will the clerk quietly say, "Yes, sir," and go do the task?

On your life he will not. He will look at you out of a fishy eye and ask one or more of the following questions:

Who was he?

Which encyclopedia?

Was I hired for that?

Where is the encyclopedia?

Don't you mean Bismarck?

What's the matter with Charlie doing it?

Is he dead?

Is there any hurry?

Sha'n't I bring you the book and let you look it up yourself?

What do you want to know for?

And I will lay you ten to one that after you have answered the questions, and explained how to find the information, and why you want it, the clerk will go off and get one of the other clerks to help him try to find Garcia—and then come back and tell you there is no such man. Of course I may lose my bet, but according to the Law of Averages I will not.

Now, if you are wise, you will not bother to explain to your "assistant" that Correggio is indexed under the C's, not in the K's, but you will smile very sweetly and say, "Never mind," and go look it up yourself. And this incapacity for independent action, this moral stupidity, this infirmity of the will, this unwillingness to cheerfully catch hold and lift—these are the things that put pure Socialism so far into the future. If men will not act for themselves, what will they do when the benefit of their effort is for all?

A first mate with knotted club seems necessary; and

the dread of getting "the bounce" Saturday night holds many a worker to his place. Advertise for a stenographer, and nine out of ten who apply can neither spell nor punctuate—and do not think it necessary to.

Can such a one write a letter to Garcia?

"You see that bookkeeper," said the foreman to me in a large factory.

"Yes; what about him?"

"Well, he's a fine accountant, but if I'd send him up town on an errand, he might accomplish the errand all right, and on the other hand, might stop at four saloons on the way, and when he got to Main Street would forget what he had been sent for."

Can such a man be entrusted to carry a message to Garcia?

We have recently been hearing much maudlin sympathy expressed for the "downtrodden denizens of the sweatshop" and the "homeless wanderer searching for honest employment," and with all often go many hard words for the men in power.

Nothing is said about the employer who grows old before his time in a vain attempt to get frowsy ne'er-do-wells to do intelligent work; and his long, patient striving after "help" that does nothing but loaf when his back is turned. In every store and factory there is a constant weeding-out process going on. The employer is constantly sending away "help" that have shown their incapacity to further the interests of the business, and others are being taken on. No matter how good times are, this sorting continues: only, if times are hard and work is scarce, the sorting is done finer—but out and forever out the incompetent and unworthy go. It is the survival of the fittest. Self-interest prompts every employer to keep the best—those who can carry a message to Garcia.

I know one man of really brilliant parts who has not the ability to manage a business of his own, and yet who is absolutely worthless to anyone else, because he carries with him constantly the insane suspicion that his employer is oppressing, or intending to oppress him. He cannot give orders, and he will not receive them. Should a message be given him to take to Garcia, his answer would probably be, "Take it yourself!"

Tonight this man walks the streets looking for work, the wind whistling through his threadbare coat. No one who knows him dares employ him, for he is a regular firebrand of discontent. He is impervious to reason, and the only thing that can impress him is the toe of a thick-soled Number Nine boot.

Of course, I know that one so morally deformed is no less to be pitied than a physical cripple; but in our pitying let us drop a tear, too, for the men who are striving to carry on a great enterprise, whose working hours are not limited by the whistle, and whose hair is fast turning white through the struggle to hold in line dowdy indifference, slipshod imbecility, and the heartless ingratitude which, but for their enterprise, would be both hungry and homeless.

Have I put the matter too strongly? Possibly I have; but when all the world has gone a-slumming I wish to speak a word of sympathy for the man who succeeds—the man who, against great odds, has directed the efforts of others, and having succeeded, finds there's nothing in it: nothing but bare board and clothes. I have carried a dinner-pail and worked for day's wages, and I have also been an employer of labor, and I know there is something to be said on both sides. There is no excellence, per se, in poverty; rags are no recommendation; and all employers are not rapacious and high-handed, any more than all poor men are virtuous. My heart goes out to the man who does his work when the "boss" is away, as well as when he is at home. And the man who, when given a letter for Garcia, quietly takes the missive, without asking any idiotic questions, and with no lurking intention of chucking it into the nearest sewer, or of doing aught else but deliver it, never gets "laid off," nor has to go on a strike for higher wages. Civilization is one long, anxious search for just such individuals. Anything such a man asks shall be granted. He is wanted in every city, town and village—in every office, shop, store and factory. The world cries out for such; he is needed and needed badly—the man who can

CARRY A MESSAGE TO GARCIA

GOOD CITIZENSHIP

Grover Cleveland

From PATRIOTISM AND HOLIDAY OBSERVANCE,
ADDRESS BEFORE THE UNION LEAGUE CLUB, CHICAGO,
FEBRUARY 22, 1907

Our country is infinitely more than a domain affording to those who dwell upon it immense material advantages and opportunities. In such a country we live. But I love to think of a glorious nation built upon the will of free men, set apart for the propagation and cultivation of humanity's best ideal of a free government, and made ready for the growth and fruitage of the highest aspirations of patriotism. This is the country that lives in us. I indulge in no mere figure of speech when I say that our nation, the immortal spirit of our domain, lives in us—in our hearts and minds and consciences. There it must find its nutriment or die. This thought more than any other presents to our minds the impressiveness and responsibility of American citizenship. The land we live in seems to be strong and active. But how fares the land that lives in us? Are we sure that we are doing all we ought to keep it in vigor and health? Are we keeping its roots well surrounded by the fertile soil of loving allegiance, and are we furnishing them the invigorating moisture of unselfish fidelity? Are we as diligent as we ought to be to protect this precious growth against the poison that must arise from the decay of harmony and honesty and industry and frugality; and are we sufficiently watchful against the deadly, burrowing pests of consuming greed and cankerous cupidity? Our answers to these questions make up the account of our stewardship as keepers of a sacred trust.

YANKS

James W. Foley

O'Leary, from Chicago, and a first-class fightin' man,
Born in County Clare or Kerry, where the gentle art began;
Sergeant Dennis P. O'Leary, from somewhere on Archie Road,
Dodgin' shells and smellin' powder while the battle ebbed and flowed.

And the captain says: "O'Leary, from your fightin' company
Pick a dozen fightin' Yankees and come skirmishin' with me;
Pick a dozen fightin' devils, and I know it's you who can,"
And O'Leary, he saluted like a first-class fightin' man.

O'Leary's eye was piercin' and O'Leary's voice was clear:
"Dimitri Georgoupoulos!" and Dimitri answered, "Here!"
Then, "Vladimir Slaminsky! Step three paces to the front,
For we're wantin' you to join us in a little Heinie hunt!"

"Garibaldi Ravioli!" Garibaldi was to share;
And, "Ole Axel Kettelson!" and, "Thomas Scalp-the-Bear!"
Who was Choctaw by inheritance, bred in the blood and bones.
But set down in army records by the name of Thomas Jones.

"Van Winkle Schuyler Stuyvesant!" Van Winkle was a bud
From the ancient tree of Stuyvesant and had it in his blood;
"Don Miguel de Colombo!" Don Miguel's next of kin
Were across the Rio Grande when Don Miguel went in.

"Ulysses Grant O'Sheridan!" Ulysses' sire, you see,
Had been at Appomattox near the famous apple tree;
And, "Patrick Michael Casey!" Patrick Michael, you can tell,
Was a fightin' man by nature with three fightin' names as well.

"Joe Wheeler Lee!" And Joseph had a pair of fightin' eyes;
And his grandad was a Johnny, as perhaps you might surmise;
Then, "Robert Bruce MacPherson!" And the Yankee squad was done
With, "Isaac Abie Cohen!" once a lightweight champion.

Then O'Leary paced 'em forward and, says he: "You Yanks, fall in!"
And he marched 'em to the captain. "Let the skirmishin' begin,"
Says he, "The Yanks are comin', and you beat 'em if you can!"
And saluted like a soldier and a first-class fightin' man!

HIGH OF HEART

Theodore Roosevelt

This is a new nation, based on a mighty continent, of boundless possibilities. No other nation in the world has such resources. No other nation has ever been so favored. If we dare to rise level to the opportunities offered us, our destiny will be vast beyond the power of imagination. We must master this destiny, and make it our own; and we can thus make it our own only if we, as a vigorous and separate nation, develop a great and wonderful nationality, distinctively different from any other nationality, of either the present or the past. For such a nation all of us can well afford to give up all other allegiances, and high of heart to stand, a mighty and united people, facing a future of glorious promise.

CONCORD HYMN

Ralph Waldo Emerson

SUNG AT THE COMPLETION OF THE
BATTLE MONUMENT, JULY 4, 1937

By the rude bridge that arched the flood,
Their flag to April's breeze unfurled,
Here once the embattled farmers stood
And fired the shot heard round the world.

The foe long since in silence slept;
Alike the conqueror silent sleeps;
And Time the ruined bridge has swept
Down the dark stream which seaward creeps.

On this green bank, by this soft stream,
We set today a votive stone;
That memory may their deed redeem,
When, like our sires, our sons are gone.

Spirit, that made those heroes dare,
To die, and leave their children free,
Bid Time and Nature gently spare
The shaft we raise to them and thee.

WHEN JOHNNY COMES MARCHING HOME

Patrick Sarsfield Gilmore

When Johnny comes marching home again,
  Hurrah! hurrah!
We'll give him a hearty welcome then,
  Hurrah! hurrah!
The men will cheer, the boys will shout,
The ladies, they will all turn out,
  And we'll all feel gay,
When Johnny comes marching home.

The old church-bell will peal with joy,
  Hurrah! hurrah!
To welcome home our darling boy,
  Hurrah! hurrah!
The village lads and lasses say,
With roses they will strew the way;
  And we'll all feel gay,
When Johnny comes marching home.

Get ready for the jubilee,
  Hurrah! hurrah!
We'll give the hero three times three,
  Hurrah! hurrah!
The laurel-wreath is ready now
To place upon his loyal brow,
  And we'll all feel gay,
When Johnny comes marching home.

Let love and friendship on that day,
  Hurrah! hurrah!
Their choicest treasures then display,
  Hurrah! hurrah!
And let each one perform some part,
To fill with joy the warrior's heart;
  And we'll all feel gay,
When Johnny comes marching home.

REVEILLÉ

Louis Untermeyer

APRIL 6, 1917

What sudden bugle calls us in the night
    And wakes us from a dream that we had shaped;
Flinging us sharply up against a fight
    We thought we had escaped?

It is no easy waking, and we win
    No final peace; our victories are few.
But still imperative forces pull us in
    And sweep us somehow through.

Summoned by a supreme and confident power
    That wakes our sleeping courage like a blow,
We rise, half-shaken, to the challenging hour,
    And answer it—and go. . . .

VICTORY BELLS

Grace Hazard Conkling

I heard the bells across the trees,
I heard them ride the plunging breeze
Above the roofs from tower and spire,
And they were leaping like a fire,
And they were shining like a stream
With sun to make its music gleam.
Deep tones as though the thunder tolled,
Cool voices thin as tinkling gold,
They shook the spangled autumn down
From out the tree-tops of the town;
They left great furrows in the air
And made a clangor everywhere
As of metallic wings. They flew
Aloft in spirals to the blue
Tall tent of heaven and disappeared.
And others, swift as though they feared
The people might not heed their cry
Went shouting Victory up the sky.
They did not say that war is done,
Only that glory has begun
Like sunrise, and the coming day
Will burn the clouds of war away.
There will be time for dreams again,
And home-coming for weary men.

WAR AGAINST GERMANY

Woodrow Wilson

It is a war against all nations. American ships have been sunk, American lives taken, in ways which it has stirred us very deeply to learn of, but the ships and people of other neutral and friendly nations have been sunk and overwhelmed in the waters in the same way. There has been no discrimination. The challenge is to all mankind. Each nation must decide for itself how it will meet it. The choice we make for ourselves must be made with a moderation of counsel and a temperateness of judgment befitting our character and our motives as a nation. We must put excited feeling away. Our motive will not be revenge or the victorious assertion of the physical might of the nation, but only the vindication of right, of human right, of which we are only a single champion.

When I addressed the Congress on the twenty-sixth of February last I thought that it would suffice to assert our neutral rights with arms, our right to use the seas against unlawful interference, our right to keep our people safe against unlawful violence. But armed neutrality, it now appears, is impracticable. Because submarines are in effect outlaws when used as the German submarines have been used against merchant shipping, it is impossible to defend ships against their attacks as the law of nations has assumed that merchantmen would defend themselves against privateers or cruisers, visible craft giving chase upon the open sea. It is common prudence in such circumstances, grim necessity indeed, to endeavour to destroy them before they have shown their own intention. They must be dealt with upon sight, if dealt with at all. The German Government denies the right of neutrals to use arms at all within the areas of the sea which it has proscribed, even in the defense of rights which no modern publicist has ever before questioned their right to defend. The intimation is conveyed that the armed guards which we have placed on our merchant ships will be treated as beyond the pale of law and subject to be dealt with as pirates would be. Armed neutrality is ineffectual enough at best; in such circumstances and in the face of such pretensions it is worse than ineffectual; it is likely only to produce what it was meant to prevent; it is practically certain to draw us into the war without either the rights or the effectiveness of belligerents. There is one choice we cannot make, we are incapable of making: we will not choose the path of submission and suffer the most sacred rights of our nation and our people to be ignored or violated. The wrongs against which we now array ourselves are no common wrongs: they cut to the very roots of human life.

With a profound sense of the solemn and even tragical character of the step I am taking and of the grave responsibilities which it involves, but in unhesitating obedience to what I deem my constitutional duty, I advise that the Congress declare the recent course of the Imperial German Government to be in fact nothing less than war against the government and people of the United States; that it formally accept the status of belligerent which has thus been thrust upon it; and that it take immediate steps not only to put the country in a more thorough state of defense but also to exert all its power and employ all its resources to bring the Government of the German Empire to terms and end the war.

We have no quarrel with the German people. We have no feeling towards them but one of sympathy and friendship. It was not upon their impulse that their government acted in entering this war. It was not with their previous knowledge or approval. It was a war determined upon as wars used to be determined upon in the old, unhappy days when peoples were nowhere consulted by their rulers and wars were provoked and waged in the interest of dynasties or of little groups of ambitious men who were accustomed to use their fellow men as pawns and tools. Self-governed nations do not fill their neighbour states with spies or set the course of intrigue to bring about some critical posture of affairs which will give them an opportunity to strike and make conquest. Such designs can be successfully worked out only under cover and where no one has the right to ask questions. Cunningly contrived plans of deception or aggression, carried, it may be, from generation to generation, can be worked out and kept from the light only within the privacy of courts or behind the carefully guarded confidences of a narrow and privileged class. They are happily impossible where public opinion commands and insists upon full information concerning all the nation's affairs.

INVOCATION

Stephen Vincent Benét

American muse, whose strong and diverse heart
So many men have tried to understand
But only made it smaller with their art,
Because you are as various as your land,

As mountainous-deep, as flowered with blue rivers,
Thirsty with deserts, buried under snows,
As native as the shape of Navajo quivers,
And native, too, as the sea-voyaged rose.

Swift runner, never captured or subdued,
Seven-branched elk beside the mountain stream,
That half a hundred hunters have pursued
But never matched their bullets with the dream,

Where the great huntsmen failed, I set my sorry
mortal snare for your immortal quarry.

You are the buffalo-ghost, the broncho-ghost
With dollar-silver in your saddle-horn,
The cowboys riding in from Painted Post,
The Indian arrow in the Indian corn,

And you are the clipped velvet of the lawns
Where Shropshire grows from Massachusetts sods,
The grey Maine rocks—and the war-painted dawns
That break above the Garden of the Gods.

The prairie-schooners crawling toward the ore
And the cheap car, parked by the station-door.

Where the skyscrapers lift their foggy plumes
Of stranded smoke out of a stony mouth
You are that high stone and its arrogant fumes,
And you are ruined gardens in the South

And bleak New England farms, so winter-white
Even their roofs look lonely, and the deep
The middle grainland where the wind of night
Is like all blind earth sighing in her sleep.

A friend, an enemy, a sacred hag
With two tied oceans in her medicine-bag.

They tried to fit you with an English song
And clip your speech into the English tale.
But, even from the first, the words went wrong,
The catbird pecked away the nightingale.

The homesick men begot high-cheekboned things
Whose wit was whittled with a different sound
And Thames and all the rivers of the kings
Ran into Mississippi and were drowned.

They planted England with a stubborn trust.
But the cleft dust was never English dust.

Stepchild of every exile from content
And all the disavouched, hard-bitten pack
Shipped overseas to steal a continent
With neither shirts nor honor to their back.

Pimping grandee and rump-faced regicide,
Apple-cheeked younkers from a windmill-square,
Puritans stubborn as the nails of Pride,
Rakes from Versailles and thieves from County
    Clare,

The black-robed priests who broke their hearts in
    vain
To make you God and France or God and Spain.

These were your lovers in your buckskin-youth
And each one married with a dream so proud
He never knew it could not be the truth
And that he coupled with a girl of cloud.

And now to see you is more difficult yet
Except as an immensity of wheel
Made up of wheels, oiled with inhuman sweat
And glittering with the heat of ladled steel.

All these you are, and each is partly you,
And none is false, and none is wholly true.

So how to see you as you really are,
So how to suck the pure, distillate, stored
Essence of essence from the hidden star
And make it pierce like a riposting sword.

For, as we hunt you down, you must escape
And we pursue a shadow of our own
That can be caught in a magician's cape
But has the flatness of a painted stone.

Never the running stag, the gull at wing,
The pure elixir, the American thing.

To strive at last, against an alien proof
And by the changes of an alien moon,
To build again that blue, American roof
Over a half-forgotten battle-tune

And call unsurely, from a haunted ground,
Armies of shadows and the shadow-sound.

I AM AN AMERICAN

Elias Lieberman

The Great War in Europe made a strong call for the exercise of American patriotism. And why should not Americans be patriotic? If the German believes that his Fatherland is of more value than life itself; if the Englishman thrills at the thought of the British Empire; if the Irishman knows no country as dear as the Emerald Isle; if the Frenchman's living and dying prayer is, *"Vive la France"*; if the Chinaman pities everybody born outside the Flowery Kingdom, and the Japanese give their sole devotion to the Land of the Rising Sun—shall not we, in this land of glorious liberty, have some thought and love of country?

At a meeting of school children in Madison Square Garden, New York City, to celebrate the Fourth of July, one boy, a descendant of native Americans, spoke as follows:

"I am an American. My father belongs to the Sons of the Revolution; my mother, to the Colonial Dames. One of my ancestors pitched tea overboard in Boston Harbor; another stood his ground with Warren; another hungered with Washington at Valley Forge. My forefathers were American in the making: they spoke in her council halls; they died on her battlefields; they commanded her ships, they cleared her forests. Dawns reddened and paled. Stanch hearts of mine beat fast at each new star in the nation's flag. Keen eyes of mine foresaw her greater glory; the sweep of her seas, the plenty of her plains, the man-hives in her billion-wired cities. Every drop of blood in me holds a heritage of patriotism. I am proud of my past. I am an American."

Then a foreign-born boy arose and said:

"I am an American. My father was an atom of dust, my mother was a straw in the wind, to His Serene Majesty. One of my ancestors died in the mines of Siberia; another was crippled for life by twenty blows of the *knout;* another was killed defending his home during the massacres. The history of my ancestors is a trail of blood to the palace-gate of the Great White Czar. But then the dream came—the dream of America. In the light of the Liberty torch the atom of dust became a man and the straw in the wind became a woman for the first time. 'See,' said my father, pointing to the flag that fluttered near, 'that flag of stars and stripes is yours; it is the emblem of the promised land. It means, my son, the hope of humanity. Live for it . . . die for it!' Under the open sky of my new country I swore to do so; and every drop of blood in me will keep that vow. I am proud of my future. I am an American."

THANKSGIVING

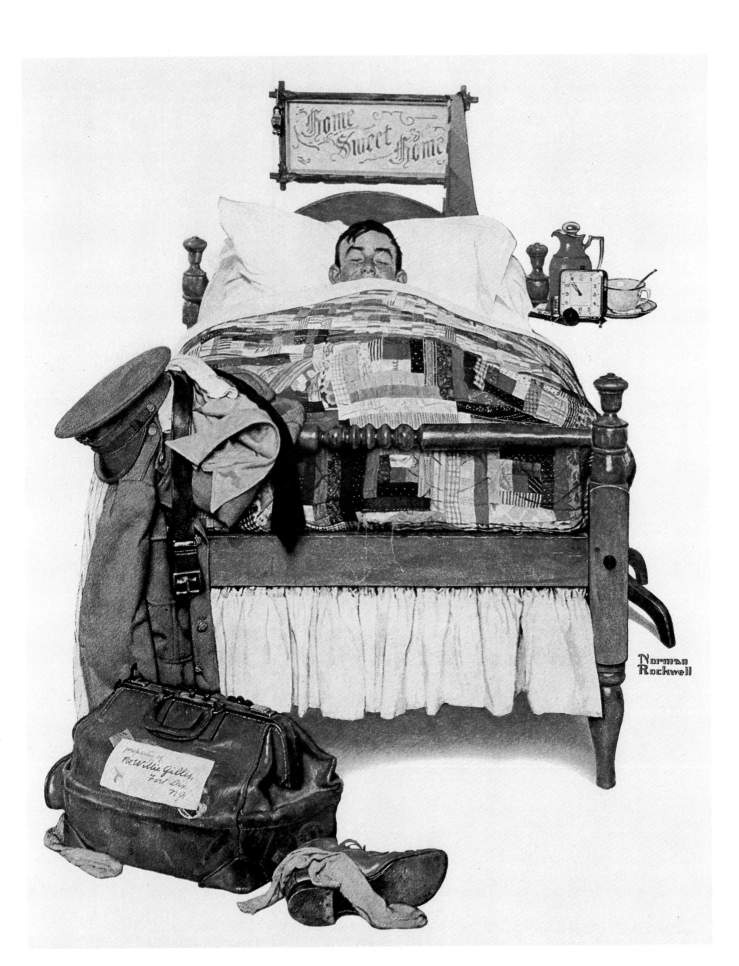

AMERICA FOR ME

Henry Van Dyke

It's fine to see the Old World, and travel up and down
Among the famous palaces and cities of renown,
To admire the crumbly castles and the statues of the kings,—
But now I think I've had enough of antiquated things.

So it's home again, and home again, America for me!
My heart is turning home again, and there I long to be
In the land of youth and freedom beyond the ocean bars,
Where the air is full of sunlight and the flag is full of stars.

Oh, London is a man's town, there's power in the air;
And Paris is a woman's town, with flowers in her hair;
And it's sweet to dream in Venice, and it's great to study Rome,
But when it comes to living, there is no place like home.

I like the German fir-woods, in green battalions drilled;
I like the gardens of Versailles with flashing fountains filled;
But, oh, to take your hand, my dear, and ramble for a day
In the friendly western woodland where Nature has her way!

I know that Europe's wonderful, yet something seems to lack!
The Past is too much with her, and the people looking back.
But the glory of the Present is to make the Future free,—
We love our land for what she is and what she is to be.

Oh, it's home again, and home again, America for me!
I want a ship that's westward bound to plough the rolling sea,
To the blessed Land of Room Enough beyond the ocean bars,
Where the air is full of sunlight and the flag is full of stars.

THE COMING AMERICAN

Sam Walter Foss

Bring me men to match my mountains,
Bring me men to match my plains,
And new eras in their brains.
Bring me men to match my prairies,
Men to match my inland seas,
Men whose thoughts shall pave a highway
Up to ampler destinies,
Pioneers to cleanse thought's marshlands,
    And to cleanse old error's fen;
Bring me men to match my mountains—
Bring me men!

Bring me men to match my forests,
Strong to fight the storm and beast,
Branching toward the skyey future,
Rooted on the futile past.
Bring me men to match my valleys,
    Tolerant of rain and snow,

Men within whose fruitful purpose
    Time's consummate blooms shall grow,
Men to tame the tigerish instincts
    Of the lair and cave and den,
Cleanse the dragon slime of nature—
    Bring me men!

Bring me men to match my rivers,
    Continent cleansers, flowing free,
Drawn by eternal madness,
    To be mingled with the sea—
Men of oceanic impulse,
    Men whose moral currents sweep
Toward the wide, infolding ocean
    Of an undiscovered deep—
Men who feel the strong pulsation
    Of the central sea, and then
Time their currents by its earth throbs—
    Bring me Men.

THE AMERICAN DREAM

James Truslow Adams

The point is that if we are to have a rich and full life in which all are to share and play their parts, if the American dream is to be a reality, our communal spiritual and intellectual life must be distinctly higher than elsewhere, where classes and groups have their separate interests, habits, markets, arts, and lives. If the dream is not to prove possible of fulfillment, we might as well become stark realists, become once more class-conscious, and struggle as individuals or classes against one another. If it is to come true, those on top, financially, intellectually, or otherwise, have got to devote themselves to the "Great Society," and those who are below in the scale have got to strive to rise, not merely economically, but culturally. We cannot become a great democracy by giving ourselves up as individuals to selfishness, physical comfort, and cheap amusements. The very foundation of the American dream of a better and richer life for all is that all, in varying degrees, shall be capable of wanting to share in it. It can never be wrought into a reality by cheap people or by "keeping up with the Joneses." There is nothing whatever in a fortune merely in itself or in a man merely in himself. It all depends on what is made of each. Lincoln was not great because he was born in a log cabin, but because he got out of it—that is, because he rose above the poverty, ignorance, lack of ambition, shiftlessness of character, contentment with mean things and low aims which kept so many thousands in the huts where they were born.

MY AMERICA

John Buchan

The United States is the richest, and, both actually and potentially, the most powerful state on the globe. She has much, I believe, to give to the world; indeed, to her hands is chiefly entrusted the shaping of the future. If democracy in the broadest and truest sense is to survive, it will be mainly because of her guardianship. For, with all her imperfections, she has a clearer view than any other people of the democratic fundamentals.

She starts from the right basis, for she combines a firm grip on the past with a quick sense of present needs and a bold outlook on the future. This she owes to her history; the combination of the British tradition with the necessities of a new land; the New England township and the Virginian manor *plus* the frontier. Much of that tradition was relinquished as irrelevant to her needs, but much remains: a talent for law which is not incompatible with a lawless practice; respect for a certain type of excellence in character which has made her great men uncommonly like our own; a disposition to compromise, but only after a good deal of arguing; an intense dislike of dictation. To these instincts the long frontier struggles added courage in the face of novelties, adaptability, enterprise, doggedness which was never lumpish, but alert and expectant.

That is the historic basis of America's democracy, and today she is the chief exponent of a creed which I believe on the whole to be the best in this imperfect world. She is the chief exponent for two reasons. The first is her size; she exhibits its technique in large type, so that he who runs may read. More important, she exhibits it in its most intelligible form, so that its constituents are obvious. Democracy has become with many an unpleasing parrot-cry, and, as I have urged elsewhere in this book, it is well to be clear what it means. It is primarily a spiritual testament, from which certain political and economic orders naturally follow. But the essence is the testament; the orders may change while the testament stands. This testament, this ideal of citizenship, she owes to no one teacher. There was a time when I fervently admired Alexander Hamilton and could not away with Jefferson; the latter only began to interest me, I think, after I had seen the University of Virginia, which he created. But I deprecate partisanship in those ultimate matters. The democratic testament derives from Hamilton as well as from Jefferson.

It has two main characteristics. The first is that the ordinary man believes in himself and in his ability, along with his fellows, to govern his country. It is when a people loses its self-confidence that it surrenders its soul to a dictator or an oligarchy. In Mr. Walter Lippmann's tremendous metaphor, it welcomes manacles to prevent its hands shaking. The second is the belief, which is fundamental also in Christianity, of the worth of every human soul—the worth, not the equality. This is partly an honest emotion, and partly a reasoned principle—that something may be made out of anybody, and that there is something likeable about everybody if you look for it—or, in canonical words, that ultimately there is nothing common or unclean.

The democratic testament is one lesson that America has to teach the world. A second is a new reading of nationalism. Some day and somehow the peoples must discover a way to brigade themselves for peace. Now, there are on the globe only two proven large-scale organisations of social units, the United States and the British Empire. The latter is not for export, and could not be duplicated; its strength depends upon a thousand-year-old monarchy and a store of unformulated traditions. But the United States was the conscious work of men's hands, and a task which has once been performed can be performed again. She is the supreme example of a federation in being, a federation which

recognises the rights and individuality of the parts, but accepts the overriding interests of the whole. To achieve this compromise she fought a desperate war. If the world is ever to have prosperity and peace, there must be some kind of federation—I will not say of democracies, but of states which accept the reign of Law. In such a task she seems to me to be the predestined leader. Vigorous as her patriotism is, she has escaped the jealous, barricadoed nationalism of the Old World. Disraeli, so often a prophet in spite of himself, in 1863, at a critical moment of the Civil War, spoke memorable words:

> There is a grave misapprehension, both in the ranks of Her Majesty's Government and of Her Majesty's Opposition, as to what constitutes the true meaning of the American democracy. The American democracy is not made up of the scum of the great industrial cities of the United States, nor of an exhausted middle class that speculates in stocks and calls that progress. The American democracy is made up of something far more stable, that may ultimately decide the fate of the two Americas and of 'Europe.'

For forty years I have regarded America not only with a student's interest in a fascinating problem, but with the affection of one to whom she has become almost a second motherland. Among her citizens I count many of my closest friends; I have known all her presidents, save one, since Theodore Roosevelt, and all her ambassadors to the Court of Saint James's since John Hay; for five years I have been her neighbour in Canada. But I am not blind to the grave problems which confront her. Democracy, after all, is a negative thing. It provides a fair field for the Good Life, but it is not in itself the Good Life. In these days when lovers of freedom may have to fight for their cause, the hope is that the ideal of the Good Life, in which alone freedom has any meaning, will acquire a stronger potency. It is the task of civilisation to raise every citizen above want, but in so doing to permit a free development and avoid the slavery of the beehive and the antheap. A humane economic policy must not be allowed to diminish the stature of man's spirit. It is because I believe that in the American people the two impulses are of equal strength that I see her in the vanguard of that slow upward trend, undulant or spiral, which today is our modest definition of progress. Her major prophet is still Whitman. 'Everything comes out of the dirt—everything; everything comes out of the people, everyday people, the people as you find them and leave them; people, people, just people!'

It is only out of the dirt that things grow.

THE FULL-FLEDGED AMERICAN

Struthers Burt

Were I to have a vision of a full-fledged American it would be something like this: A man who, with sufficient knowledge of the past, would walk fairly constantly with the thought that he was blood-brother, if not by actual race then by the equally subtle method of mental vein transfusing into mental vein, of Washington and Lincoln; of Jefferson and Lee, and of all the men like them. Who would walk, because of this, carefully and proudly, and also humbly, lest he fail them. And, with a keen sense of the present and the future, would say to himself: "I am an American and therefore what I do, however small, is of importance."

Never in history have the times been more ripe for a sober discussion, a deep contemplation, of the kind of patriotism I imply. The American citizen is no longer a frontiersman; he can no longer make a mission here and lose it there, and go on and make a million somewhere else, and meanwhile let his country take care of itself. The American is no longer a colonial, even in retrospect. Circumstances are forcing him into a deep, straight, independent form of thinking.

Pseudo-patriotism may be the last refuge of a scoundrel, but it is beginning to be apparent that before long, real patriotism, as so often before in history, will be not only the last, and only possible, refuge of the intelligent and far-visioned citizen, but also his sword, his rallying cry, and the emblem of his advance.

FLAG DAY–1940

THE NEW YORK TIMES,
JUNE 14, 1940

What's a flag? What's the love of country for which it stands? Maybe it begins with love of the land itself. It is the fog rolling in with the tide at Eastport, or through the Golden Gate and among the towers of San Francisco. It is the sun coming up behind the White Mountains, over the Green, throwing a shining glory on Lake Champlain and above the Adirondacks. It is the storied Mississippi rolling swift and muddy past St. Louis, rolling past Cairo, pouring down past the levees of New Orleans. It is lazy noontide in the pines of Carolina, it is a sea of wheat rippling in western Kansas, it is the San Francisco peaks far north across the glowing nakedness of Arizona, it is the Grand Canyon and a little stream coming down out of a New England ridge, in which are trout.

It is men at work. It is the storm-tossed fishermen coming into Gloucester and Providence and Astoria. It is the farmer riding his great machine in the dust of harvest, the dairyman going to the barn before sunrise, the lineman mending the broken wire, the miner drilling for the blast. It is the servants of fire in the murky splendor of Pittsburgh, between the Allegheny and the Monogahela, the trucks rumbling through the night, the locomotive engineer bringing the train in on time, the pilot in the clouds, the riveter running along the beam a hundred feet in air. It is the clerk in the office, the housewife doing the dishes and sending the children off to school. It is the teacher, doctor and parson tending and helping, body and soul, for small reward.

It is small things remembered, the little corners of the land, the houses, the people that each one loves. We love our country because there was a little tree on a hill, and grass thereon, and a sweet valley below; because the hurdy-gurdy man came along on a sunny morning in a city street; because a beach or a farm or a lane or a house that might not seem much to others were once, for each of us, made magic. It is voices that are remembered only, no longer heard. It is parents, friends, the lazy chat of street and store and office, and the ease of mind that makes life tranquil. It is Summer and Winter, rain and sun and storm. These are flesh of our flesh, bone of our bone, blood of our blood, a lasting part of what we are, each of us and all of us together.

It is stories told. It is the Pilgrims dying in their first dreadful Winter. It is the minute man standing his ground at Concord Bridge, and dying there. It is the army in rags, sick, freezing, starving at Valley Forge. It is the wagons and the men on foot going westward over Cumberland Gap, floating down the great rivers, rolling over the great plains. It is the settler hacking fiercely at the primeval forest on his new, his own lands. It is Thoreau at Walden Pond,

Lincoln at Cooper Union, and Lee riding home from Appomattox. It is corruption and disgrace, answered always by men who would not let the flag lie in the dust, who have stood up in every generation to fight for the old ideals and the old rights, at risk of ruin or of life itself.

It is a great multitude of people on pilgrimage, common and ordinary people, charged with the usual human failings, yet filled with such a hope as never caught the imaginations and the hearts of any nation on earth before. The hope of liberty. The hope of justice. The hope of a land in which a man can stand straight, without fear, without rancor.

The land and the people and the flag—the land a continent, the people of every race, the flag a symbol of what humanity may aspire to when the wars are over and the barriers are down; to these each generation must be dedicated and consecrated anew, to defend with life itself, if need be, but, above all, in friendliness, in hope, in courage, to live for.

Thanksgiving
norman rockwell

THE AMERICAN CHARACTER

George Santayana

At the same time, the American is imaginative; for where life is intense, imagination is intense also. Were he not imaginative he would not live so much in the future. But his imagination is practical, and the future it forecasts is immediate; it works with the clearest and least ambiguous terms known to his experience, in terms of number, measure, contrivance, economy, and speed. He is an idealist working on matter. Understanding as he does the material potentialities of things, he is successful in invention, conservative in reform, and quick in emergencies. All his life he jumps into the train after it has started and jumps out before it has stopped; and he never once gets left behind, or breaks a leg. There is an enthusiasm in his sympathetic handling of material forces which goes far to cancel the illiberal character which it might otherwise assume. The good workman hardly distinguishes his artistic intention from the potency in himself and in things which is about to realize that intention. Accordingly his ideals fall into the form of premonitions and prophecies; and his studious prophecies often come true. So do the happy workmanlike ideals of the American. When a poor boy, perhaps, he dreams of an education, or at least a degree; he dreams of growing rich, and he grows rich—only more slowly and modestly, perhaps, than he expected; he dreams of marrying his Rebecca and, even if he marries a Leah instead, he ultimately finds in Leah his Rebecca after all. He dreams of helping to carry on and to accelerate the movement of a vast, seething, progressive society, and he actually does so. Ideals clinging so close to nature are almost sure of fulfilment; the American beams with a certain self-confidence and sense of mastery; he feels that God and nature are working with him.

IN THE GREEN MOUNTAIN COUNTRY

Clarence Day

He got up at seven as usual, and he and his wife had breakfast together. At half past eight he went to his office in the town. His old friend and partner was already there when he entered. They were both early risers. They spoke with each other for a moment and then he went to his desk.

He was not feeling quite well. He said nothing about it. He had no idea that this was his last day of life.

There were a number of letters and other matters for him to go over and settle. He went to work methodically at them. He disliked to leave things undone. All his life he had attended to his duties, large or small, systematically. He was a sound, seasoned New Englander of sixty, and he had accomplished a lot.

By ten o'clock he had finished. He still wasn't feeling any better. He said to his secretary, "Mr. Ross, I guess we'll go to the house."

They motored back together through the streets and under the bare, spreading trees, till they came to the beeches and elms that surrounded his home. He had lived in half of a two-family house most of his life, but it had no grounds around it, and when he was fifty-eight he had moved; "so the doggies can have a place to play," he had said.

His wife was out—she had gone downtown on foot to do some shopping. He and his secretary went to the library. He toyed with a jigsaw puzzle a moment. They spoke of the partridge hunting they had had in October, and of the hay fever that had bothered him in July—a "pollen attack" he called it. He made little of it. He had been lucky—he had had very few illnesses.

As they sat there talking he said he was thirsty. The cook and maid were at hand, and so was Mr. Ross, but he didn't like to be waited on—he went to the kitchen and got a glass of water himself. He heard the gardener in the cellar and he went down there to say something to him. The gardener was the last man he spoke to. When people asked him later what his employer had said he couldn't remember. He told them that it was something about the house or the grounds, and that it had not seemed important—to him.

Leaving the gardener this man went upstairs to his bedroom. He took off his coat and waistcoat to shave, but sank to the floor. He was dead.

The news spread through the town. Children on their way home from school stopped to look through the gates. A few policemen arrived. When

reporters and camera men came the Chief of Police took them aside and asked them not to bother the family. He left one policeman on guard and everyone else went away.

The flag on the schoolhouse had been lowered. Now, on all public buildings, other flags went to half-mast. In town after town, and city after city, the flags fluttered down.

The next day the guns began booming. For thousands of miles throughout the nation, and at its army posts over-seas, at half hour intervals all day long, cannon by cannon they spoke. And when evening came and the bugles had sounded retreat, there were last, long, slow salutes everywhere of forty-eight guns, one for each of the forty-eight States of his country.

The hotel in Northampton was crowded that night. Friends of his had arrived for the funeral, and there were many reporters. The reporters swapped stories of the days before he had retired. One time when he had been suddenly needed, they said, for some national conference, and when nobody knew where he was, he had been found down in the storeroom, fishing a pickle out of a jar with two fingers. He had liked homemade pickles and people had sent him quantities of them, but he never got any at table, they were all kept on shelves in the storeroom, because of the chance that cranks might send jars that were poisoned.

Early in the morning the long special trains came rolling in. The President and his wife, the Vice-President, the Chief Justice, several Cabinet members, and committees of Senators and Congressmen got out of the sleeping cars from Washington and walked through the crowd at the station. Governors of near-by States and other officials arrived in their motors. They went to the Congregational Church and sat in its plain oak pews.

The service was brief. There was no eulogy, no address of any kind. Two hymns were sung, parts of the Bible were read, and the young minister prayed. He rose, and gave the great of the land who stood before him his blessing. They filed slowly out.

The streets emptied as the visitors left. The motors and trains rolled away.

When the town was alone with its own again, six sober-faced policemen lifted the coffin and carried it out to the street. Light rain was falling. Drops glistened on the coffin as it was placed in the hearse. A few motors fell in behind it, and the little procession moved off along the old country roads.

In every village they went through, there were small troops of boy scouts and veterans of the great war, standing at attention in silence as the motors sped by. In the yards of factories and mills, workmen stood in groups, waiting. Men held their hats or caps to their hearts, women folded their hands. Farms and fields on the road had been tidied up, as a mark of respect, and at a place where carpenters were building a house they had cleared away the lumber and chips.

90

The rain stopped for a while. The mists that had drifted low over the mountains gave place to blue sky. White, straight birch trunks glistened, and ice began to melt in the sunshine. But as they drove on, deeper into the Green Mountain country, black clouds spread and rain fell again, harder. The red tail lights of the cars gleamed on the road in the wintry and dark afternoon.

When the cars reached the end of the journey, the skies lightened palely a moment. The burying ground was outside the village where the dead man was born. Generations of his ancestors had been laid to rest there, in graves on the hillside. The cars climbed the steep road and stopped. The family and a handful of friends got out and stood waiting.

Across the road, in a rocky field, the men and women of the village had gathered. They were not the kind of people to intrude or crowd nearer, and they kept complete silence. The young minister said a few words as the coffin was lowered. A sudden storm of hail pelted down.

The widow, who had tried to smile that morning coming out of the church, could no longer hold back her tears.

The cars left. The bent-shouldered sexton signaled to his helpers. They filled in the grave. Four country militiamen took up their positions on guard. Snow fell that night on the hillside and the slopes of Salt Ash Mountain.

The headstone that now marks the quiet spot bears no inscription but the name, Calvin Coolidge, the dates, and the President's seal.

THE STAR-SPANGLED BANNER

Francis Scott Key

O! say, can you see, by the dawn's early light,
   What so proudly we hailed at the twilight's last gleaming:
Whose broad stripes and bright stars, through the perilous fight,
   O'er the ramparts we watched were so gallantly streaming,
And the rocket's red glare, the bombs bursting in air,
Gave proof through the night that our flag was still there;

   O! say, does the Star-Spangled Banner still wave
   O'er the land of the free and the home of the brave?

On the shore, dimly seen through the mist of the deep,
   Where the foe's haughty host in dread silence reposes,
What is that which the breeze, o'er the towering steep,
   As it fitfully blows, half conceals, half discloses?
Now it catches the gleam of the morning's first beam—
In full glory reflected, now shines on the stream;

   'Tis the Star-Spangled Banner, O! long may it wave
   O'er the land of the free and the home of the brave.

And where is the band who so vauntingly swore
   That the havoc of war and the battle's confusion
A home and a country would leave us no more?
   Their blood has washed out their foul footsteps' pollution.
No refuge could save the hireling and slave
From the terror of flight or the gloom of the grave!

   And the Star-Spangled Banner in triumph doth wave
   O'er the land of the free and the home of the brave.

O! thus be it ever when freemen shall stand
   Between their loved homes and the foe's desolation;
Bless'd with victory and peace, may our Heaven-rescued land
   Praise the Power that hath made and preserved us a nation.
Then conquer we must, for our cause it is just—
   And this be our motto—"In God is our trust!"

   And the Star-Spangled Banner in triumph shall wave
   O'er the land of the free and the home of the brave.

COLUMBIA

Timothy Dwight

Columbia, Columbia, to glory arise,
The queen of the world, and the child of the skies;
Thy genius commands thee; with rapture behold,
While ages on ages thy splendor unfold,
Thy reign is the last, and the noblest of time,
Most fruitful thy soil, most inviting thy clime;
Let the crimes of the east ne'er encrimson thy name,
Be freedom, and science, and virtue thy fame.

To conquest and slaughter let Europe aspire;
Whelm nations in blood, and wrap cities in fire;
Thy heroes the rights of mankind shall defend,
And triumph pursue them, and glory attend.
A world is thy realm: for a world be thy laws,
Enlarged as thine empire, and just as thy cause;
On Freedom's broad basis, that empire shall rise,
Extend with the main, and dissolve with the skies.

Fair science her gates to thy sons shall unbar,
And the east see the morn hide the beams of her star.
New bards, and new sages, unrivalled shall soar
To fame unextinguished, when time is no more;
To thee, the last refuge of virtue designed,
Shall fly from all nations the best of mankind;
Here, grateful to heaven, with transport shall bring
Their incense, more fragrant than odors of spring,

Nor less shall thy fair ones to glory ascend,
And genius and beauty in harmony blend;
The graces of form shall awake pure desire,
And the charms of the soul ever cherish the fire;
Their sweetness unmingled, their manners refined,
And virtue's bright image, instamped on the mind,
With peace and soft rapture shall teach life to glow,
And light up a smile in the aspect of woe.

Thy fleets to all regions thy power shall display,
The nations admire and the ocean obey;
Each shore to thy glory its tribute unfold,
And the east and the south yield their spices and gold.
As the day-spring unbounded, thy splendor shall flow,
And earth's little kingdoms before thee shall bow;
While the ensigns of union, in triumph unfurled,
Hush the tumult of war and give peace to the world.

Thus, as down a lone valley, with cedars o'erspread,
From war's dread confusion I pensively strayed,
The gloom from the face of fair heaven retired;
The winds ceased to murmur; the thunders expired;
Perfumes as of Eden flowed sweetly along,
And a voice as of angels, enchantingly sung:
"Columbia, Columbia, to glory arise,
The queen of the world, and the child of the skies."

Norman Rockwell

HAIL! COLUMBIA

Joseph Hopkinson

Hail! Columbia, happy land!
Hail! ye heroes, heav'n-born band,
Who fought and bled in freedom's cause,
Who fought and bled in freedom's cause,
And when the storm of war was gone,
Enjoyed the peace your valor won;
Let independence be your boast,
Ever mindful what it cost,
Ever grateful for the prize,
Let its altar reach the skies.

　　Chorus—Firm, united let us be,
　　　　　　Rallying round our liberty,
　　　　　　As a band of brothers joined,
　　　　　　Peace and safety we shall find.

Immortal patriots, rise once more!
Defend your rights, defend your shore;
Let no rude foe with impious hand,
Let no rude foe with impious hand
Invade the shrine where sacred lies
Of toil and blood the well-earned prize;
While offering peace, sincere and just,
In heav'n we place a manly trust,
That truth and justice may prevail,
And ev'ry scheme of bondage fail.

Sound, sound the trump of fame!
Let Washington's great name
Ring thro' the world with loud applause!
Ring thro' the world with loud applause!
Let ev'ry clime to freedom dear
Listen with a joyful ear;
With equal skill, with steady pow'r,
He governs in the fearful hour
Of horrid war, or guides with ease
The happier time of honest peace.

Behold the chief, who now commands,
Once more to serve his country stands,
The rock on which the storm will beat!
The rock on which the storm will beat!
But armed in virtue, firm and true,
His hopes are fixed on heav'n and you.
When hope was sinking in dismay,
When gloom obscured Columbia's day,
His steady mind, from changes free,
Resolved on death or liberty.

From GERMAN-AMERICANS

George S. Kaufman and Moss Hart

IRMA

No, No, Martin, I cannot tear these people out of my heart, just because now there is a war. I was born in Germany, Martin. I grew up there. So did you. I love this country—yes, but I love Germany too. I cannot help that. It is deep inside of me. My heart breaks enough when I think that these two countries I love must fight each other. But that Karl should go over there, a gun in his hand, and kill those people I grew up with—that I cannot stand.

MARTIN

Don't you think that I am tortured too, Irma? When I wake in the night and hear you crying beside me, don't you think *my* heart breaks? I love Germany too, Irma. Do you think I can forget the little town that we were born in? My mother and father, those boys and girls we went to school with—they must have sons now too, Irma, like our Karl. Do you think I *want* him to go over and kill those people?

IRMA

Then for God's sake, Martin, do not let Karl go! Do not let him go!

MARTIN

No, Irma—Karl *must* go. This country opened its arms to us, reared our children. Everything that we have and everything that we are, we owe to America. Lisa's baby is an American; the children that Karl will have will be Americans, and I am an American, Irma. And so are you!

IRMA

(Brokenly)
No, no! Don't let him go, Martin. Please! Please!

MARTIN

Irma Liebchen, he must go. This is our country, Irma, and I am proud that we *have* a son to go. We cannot divide our allegiance, Irma—we are either Germans or we are Americans, and I say we are Americans!

AMERICA

Samuel Francis Smith

My country, 'tis of thee,
Sweet Land of liberty,
   Of thee I sing;
Land where my fathers died,
Land of the Pilgrims' pride;
From every mountain side,
   Let freedom ring.

My native country, thee—
Land of the noble free—
   Thy name I love;
I love thy rocks and rills,
Thy woods and templed hills;
My heart with rapture thrills,
   Like that above.

Let music swell the breeze,
And ring from all the trees
   Sweet freedom's song;
Let mortal tongues awake;
Let all that breathe partake;
Let rocks their silence break—
   The sound prolong.

Our father's God, to thee,
Author of liberty,
   To Thee we sing;
Long may our land be bright
With freedom's holy light:
Protect us by Thy might,
   Great God, our King.

AMERICA THE BEAUTIFUL

Katharine Lee Bates

O beautiful for spacious skies,
   For amber waves of grain,
For purple mountain majesties
   Above the fruited plain!
America! America!
   God shed His grace on thee
And crown thy good with brotherhood
   From sea to shining sea!

O beautiful for pilgrim feet,
   Whose stern, impassioned stress
A thoroughfare for freedom beat
   Across the wilderness!
America! America!
   God mend thine every flaw,
Confirm thy soul in self-control,
   Thy liberty in law!

O beautiful for heroes proved
   In liberating strife,
Who more than self their country loved,
   And mercy more than life!
America! America!
   May God thy gold refine,
Till all success be nobleness
   And every gain divine!

O beautiful for patriot dream
   That sees beyond the years
   Thine alabaster cities gleam
   Undimmed by human tears!
America! America!
   God shed His grace on thee,
And crown thy good with brotherhood
   From sea to shining sea!

THE PATRIOT HYMN

Nathan Haskell Dole

Oh, country, fair and grand,
Our glorious Fatherland,
    Superb, star-crowned—
By Freedom's breezes fanned,
Firm in thy mountain band,
That guard on every hand
    Thy sacred ground!

Thy children come to-day
A wreath of love to lay
    Before thy feet.
In festival array,
With jocund hearts and gay,
Our homage pure we pay;
    With song we meet!

In War's hard Wilderness,
With bitter storm and stress,
    We've tarried long.

Now Peace thy sons shall bless!
Freedom and Righteousness
    Shall make them strong!

Strong in the cause of Right
To aid the weak with might
    Born of the Truth;
Strong as the hosts of Light
Arrayed against the Night,
To put all wrong to flight
    With zeal of Youth!

We are thy Sword and Shield!
To thee our all we yield
    At thy command.
But when War's wounds are healed,
In workshop and in field,
Our love is best revealed,
    Dear Native Land!

OUR COUNTRY

Julia Ward Howe

On primal rocks she wrote her name;
  Her towers were reared on holy graves;
The golden seed that bore her came
  Swift-winged with prayer o'er ocean waves.

The Forest bowed his solemn crest,
  And open flung his sylvan doors;
Meek Rivers led the appointed guest
  To clasp the wide-embracing shores;

Till, fold by fold, the broidered land
  To swell her virgin vestments grew,
While sages, strong in heart and hand,
  Her virtue's fiery girdle drew.

O Exile of the wrath of kings!
  O Pilgrim Ark of Liberty!
The refuge of divinest things,
  Their record must abide in thee!

First in the glories of thy front
  Let the crown-jewel, Truth, be found;
Thy right hand fling, with generous wont,
  Love's happy chain to farthest bound!

Let Justice, with the faultless scales,
  Hold fast the worship of thy sons;
Thy Commerce spread her shining sails
  Where no dark tide of rapine runs!

So link thy ways to those of God,
  So follow firm the heavenly laws,
That stars may greet thee, warrior-browed,
  And storm-sped angels hail thy cause!

O Lord, the measure of our prayers,
  Hope of the world in grief and wrong,
Be thine the tribute of the years,
  The gift of Faith, the crown of Song!

THIS IS AMERICA

Katharine Janeway Conger

This is America, these quiet hills
So still and green beneath the summer sun,
Where not one clod by violence is upturned,
Nor one tree riven by a distant gun.

This is America, these wide, rich fields,
Golden with grain and hazy in the heat;
Only the farmer's hand shall mow them down,
Nor find one body lying in the wheat.

This is America, these sandy shores
Whence every day the fishers sail again,
Nor scan the skies for threat of sudden death
Fearing no enemy save wind and rain.

This is America—O happy land
Upon whose hills and plains God's peace is shed,
God keep thee still the same, a haven where,
Except in love, no alien foot shall tread.

I HEAR AMERICA SINGING

Walt Whitman

I hear America singing, the varied carols I hear,
Those of mechanics, each one singing his as it should be blithe and
        strong,
The carpenter singing his as he measures his plank or beam,
The mason singing his as he makes ready for work, or leaves off
        work,
The boatman singing what belongs to him in his boat, the deck-
        hand singing on the steamboat deck,
The shoemaker singing as he sits on his bench, the hatter singing
        as he stands,
The wood-cutter's song, the ploughboy's on his way in the morn-
        ing, or at noon intermission or at sundown,
The delicious singing of the mother, or of the young wife at work,
        or of the girl sewing or washing,
Each singing what belongs to him or her and to none else,
The day what belongs to the day—at night the party of young
        fellows, robust, friendly,
Singing with open mouths their strong melodious songs.

THE BETTER WAY

Susan Coolidge

Who serves his country best?
Not he who, for a brief and stormy space,
Leads forth her armies to the fierce affray.
Short is the time of turmoil and unrest,
Long years of peace succeed it and replace:
There is a better way.

Who serves his country best?
Not he who guides her senates in debate,
And makes the laws which are her prop and stay;
Not he who wears the poet's purple vest
And sings her songs of love and grief and fate:
There is a better way.

He serves his country best,
Who joins the tide that lifts her nobly on;
For speech has myriad tongues for every day,
And song but one; and law within the breast
Is stronger than the graven law on stone:
This is a better way.

He serves his country best
Who lives pure life, and doeth righteous deed,
And walks straight paths, however others stray,
And leaves his sons as uttermost bequest
A stainless record which all men may read:
This is the better way.

No drop but serves the slowly lifting tide,
No dew but has an errand to some flower,
No smallest star but sheds some helpful ray,
And man by man, each giving to all the rest,
Makes the firm bulwark of the country's power:
There is no better way.

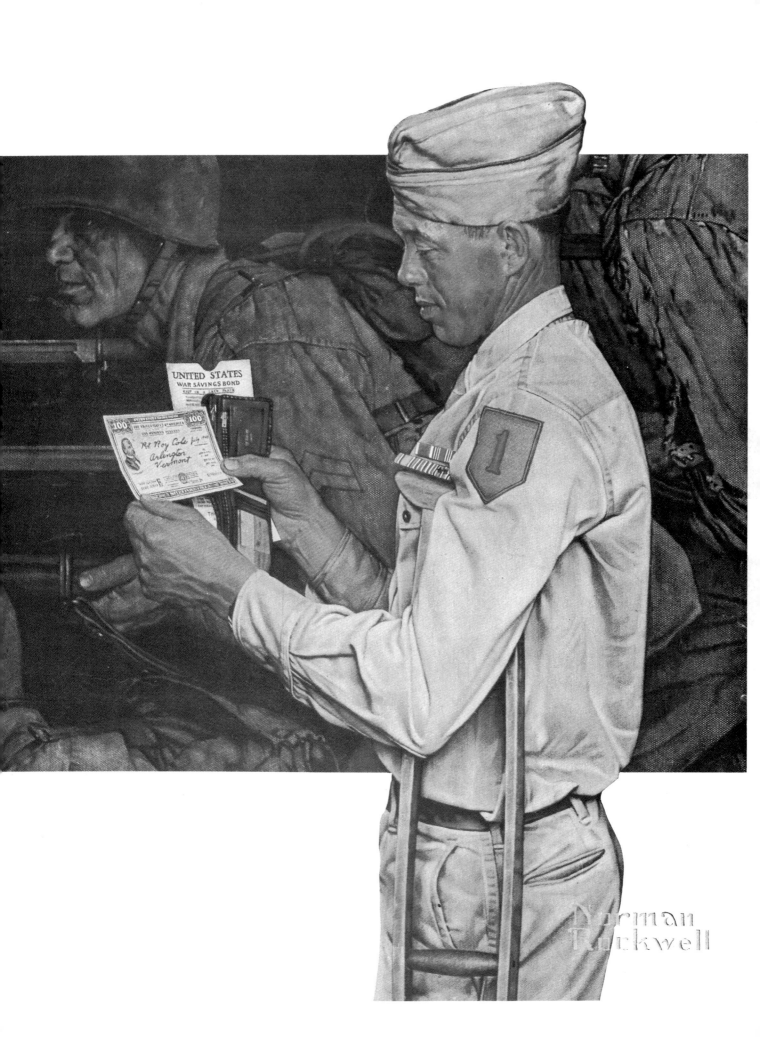

INSCRIPTION ON THE STATUE OF LIBERTY

Emma Lazarus

GIVE ME YOUR TIRED, YOUR POOR,
YOUR HUDDLED MASSES YEARNING TO BREATHE FREE,
THE WRETCHED REFUSE OF YOUR TEEMING SHORE,
SEND THESE, THE HOMELESS, TEMPEST-TOSSED, TO ME:
I LIFT MY LAMP BESIDE THE GOLDEN DOOR.

AMERICA

Sydney Dobell

Nor force nor fraud shall sunder us! Oh ye
Who north or south, on east or western land,
Native to noble sounds, say truth for truth,
Freedom for freedom, love for love, and God
For God; oh ye who in eternal youth
Speak with a living and creative flood
This universal English, and do stand
Its breathing book; live worthy of that grand
Heroic utterance—parted, yet a whole,
Far, yet unsevered—children brave and free
Of the great Mother-tongue, and ye shall be
Lords of an empire wide as Shakespeare's soul,
Sublime as Milton's immemorial theme,
And rich as Chaucer's speech, and fair as Spenser's dream.

From THE BUILDING OF THE SHIP

Henry Wadsworth Longfellow

Thou, too, sail on, O Ship of State!
Sail on, O Union, strong and great!
Humanity with all its fears,
With all the hopes of future years,
Is hanging breathless on thy fate!
We know what Master laid thy keel,
What Workmen wrought thy ribs of steel,
Who made each mast, and sail, and rope,
What anvils rang, what hammers beat,
In what a forge and what a heat
Were shaped the anchors of thy hope.
Fear not each sudden sound and shock,
'Tis of the wave and not the rock;
'Tis but the flapping of the sail,
And not a rent made by the gale!
In spite of rock and tempest's roar,
In spite of false lights on the shore,
Sail on, nor fear to breast the sea!
Our hearts, our hopes, are all with thee,
Our hearts, our hopes, our prayers, our tears,
Our faith triumphant o'er our fears,
Are all with thee,—are all with thee!

FREEDOM

James Russell Lowell

Are we, then, wholly fallen? Can it be
That thou, North wind, that from thy mountains
    bringest
Their spirit to our plains, and thou, blue sea,
Who on our rocks thy wreaths of freedom flingest,
As on an altar,—can it be that ye
Have wasted inspiration on dead ears,
Dulled with the too familiar clank of chains?
The people's heart is like a harp for years
Hung where some petrifying torrent rains
Its slow-incrusting spray: the stiffened chords
Faint and more faint make answer to the tears
That drip upon them: idle are all words:
Only a golden plectrum wakes the tone
Deep buried 'neath that ever-thickening stone.

We are not free: doth Freedom, then, consist
In musing with our faces toward the Past,
While petty cares, and crawling interests, twist
Their spider-threads about us, which at last
Grow strong as iron chains, to cramp and bind
In formal narrowness heart, soul, and mind?
Freedom is re-created year by year,
In hearts wide open on the Godward side,
In souls calm-cadenced as the whirling sphere,
In minds that sway the future like a tide.
No broadest creeds can hold her, and no codes;
She chooses men for her august abodes,
Building them fair and fronting to the dawn;
Yet, when we seek her, we but find a few
Light footprints, leading morn-ward through the
    dew:
Before the day had risen, she was gone.

And we must follow: swiftly runs she on,
And, if our steps should slacken in despair,
Half turns her face, half smiles through golden
    hair,
Forever yielding, never wholly won:
That is not love which pauses in the race
Two close-linked names on fleeting sand to trace;
Freedom gained yesterday is no more ours;
Men gather but dry seeds of last year's flowers;
Still there's a charm ungranted, still a grace,
Still rosy Hope, the free, the unattained,
Makes us Possession's languid hand let fall;
'Tis but a fragment of ourselves is gained,
The Future brings us more, but never all.

And, as the finder of some unknown realm,
Mounting a summit whence he thinks to see
On either side of him the imprisoning sea,
Beholds, above the clouds that overwhelm
The valley-land, peak after snowy peak
Stretch out of sight, each like a silver helm
Beneath its plume of smoke, sublime and
    bleak,
And what he thought an island finds to be
A continent to him first oped,—so we
Can from our height of Freedom look along
A boundless future, ours if we be strong;
Or if we shrink, better remount our ships
And, fleeing God's express design, trace back
The hero-freighted *Mayflower's* prophet-track
To Europe, entering her blood-red eclipse.

Great Great Great Grandpa Gillis

Great Great Grandpa Gillis

Great Grandpa Gillis

"Fighting Bill" Gillis

Grandpa Gillis

Gillis

your son
Willie Gillis

norman
rockwell

Victory
with
GILLIS

GREAT
AMERICAN
HEROES

The
GILLIS
FAMILY
Genealogy

Great Loves
of the
GILLISES

A HISTORY
OF THE
UNITED STATES
AND THE
GILLIS FAMILY

A HISTORY
OF THE
UNITED STATES
AND THE
GILLIS FAMILY

GILLIS
at
GETTYSBURG

Gillis
and
Lincoln

STORIES

GILLIS

FOR YOU, O DEMOCRACY

Walt Whitman

Come, I will make the continent indissoluble,
I will make the most splendid race the sun ever shone upon,
I will make divine magnetic lands,
     With the love of comrades,
        With the life-long love of comrades.

I will plant companionship thick as trees along the rivers of
     America, and along the shores of the great lakes, and all over
     the prairies,

I will make inseparable cities with their arms about each other's
     necks,
     By the love of comrades,
        By the manly love of comrades,

For you these from me, O Democracy, to serve you ma femme!
For you, for you I am trilling these songs.

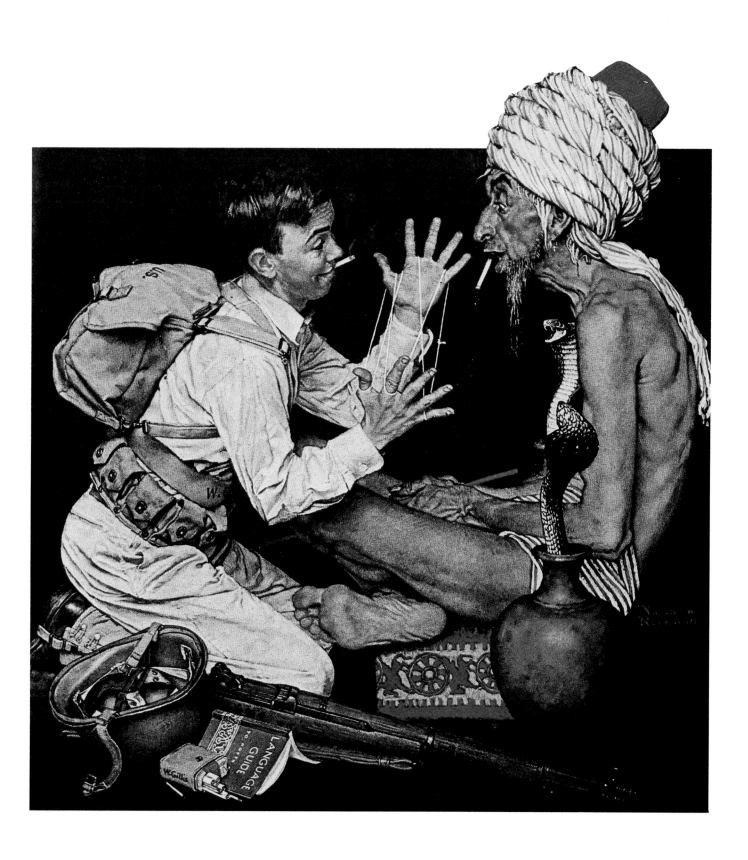

PREAMBLE TO THE CONSTITUTION OF THE UNITED STATES

We, the people of the United States, in order to form a more perfect union, establish justice, insure domestic tranquillity, provide for the common defence, promote the general welfare, and secure the blessings of liberty to ourselves and our posterity, do ordain and establish this CONSTITUTION for the United States of America.

THE NATIONAL FLAG

Henry Ward Beecher

EXTRACT FROM ADDRESS IN
PLYMOUTH CHURCH, MAY 1861

From the earliest periods nations seem to have gone forth to war under some banner. Sometimes it has been merely the pennon of a leader, and was only a rallying signal. So, doubtless, began the habit of carrying banners, to direct men in the confusion of conflict, that the leader might gather his followers around him when he himself was liable to be lost out of their sight.

Later in the history of nations the banner acquired other uses and peculiar significance from the parties, the orders, the houses, or governments, that adopted it. At length, as consolidated governments drank up into themselves all these lesser independent authorities, banners became significant chiefly of national authority. And thus in our day every people has its peculiar flag. There is no civilized nation without its banner.

A thoughtful mind, when it sees a nation's flag, sees not the flag, but the nation itself. And whatever may be its symbols, its insignia, he reads chiefly in the flag the government, the principles, the truths, the history, that belong to the nation that sets it forth. When the French tricolor rolls out to the wind, we see France. When the new-found Italian flag is unfurled, we see resurrected Italy. When the other three-colored Hungarian flag shall be lifted to the wind, we shall see in it the long buried, but never dead, principles of Hungarian liberty. When the united crosses of St. Andrew and St. George, on a fiery ground, set forth the banner of Old England, we see not the cloth merely; there rises up before the mind the idea of that great monarchy.

This nation has a banner, too, and . . . wherever it [has] streamed abroad men saw daybreak bursting on their eyes. For . . . the American flag has been a symbol of Liberty, and men rejoiced in it. Not another flag on the globe had such an errand, or went forth upon the sea carrying everywhere, the world around, such hope to the captive, and such glorious tidings. The stars upon it were to the pining nations like the bright morning stars of God, and the stripes upon it were beams of morning light. As at early dawn the stars shine forth even while it grows light, and then as the sun advances that light breaks into banks and streaming lines of color, the glowing red and intense white striving together, and ribbing the horizon with bars effulgent, so, on the American flag, stars and beams of many-colored light shine out together. And wherever this flag comes, and men behold it, they see in its sacred emblazonry no ramping lion, and no fierce eagle; no embattled castles, or insignia of imperial authority; they see the symbols of light. It is the banner of dawn. It means Liberty; and the galley-slave, the poor, oppressed conscript, the trodden-down creature of foreign despotism, sees in the American flag that very promise and prediction of God,—"The people which sat in darkness saw a great light; and to them which sat in the region and shadow of death light is sprung up."

Is this a mere fancy? On the 4th of July, 1776, the Declaration of American Independence was confirmed and promulgated. Already for more than a year the colonies had been at war with the mother country. But until this time there had been no American flag. The flag of the mother country covered us during all our colonial period; and each state that chose had a separate and significant state banner.

In 1777, within a few days of one year after the Declaration of Independence, and two years and more after the war began, upon the 14th of June, the Congress of the colonies, or the confederated states, assembled, and ordained this glorious national flag which now we hold and defend, and advanced it full high before God and all men as the flag of Liberty. It was no holiday flag, gorgeously emblazoned for gaiety or vanity. It was a solemn national signal. When that banner first unrolled to the sun, it was the symbol of all those holy truths and purposes which brought together the colonial American Congress.

Consider the men who devised and set forth this banner. The Rutledges, the Pinckneys, the Jays, the Franklins, the Hamiltons, the Jeffersons, the Adamses, —these men were all either officially connected with it or consulted concerning it. They were men that had taken their lives in their hands, and consecrated all their worldly possessions—for what? For the doctrines, and for the personal fact, of liberty,—for the right of *all* men to liberty. They had just given forth to a world a Declaration of Facts and Faiths out of which sprung the Constitution, and on which they now planted this new-devised flag of our Union.

If one, then, asks me the meaning of our flag, I say to him, It means just what Concord and Lexington meant, what Bunker Hill meant; it means the whole glorious Revolutionary War, which was, in short, the rising up of a valiant young people against an old tyranny, to establish the most momentous doctrine that the world had ever known, or has since known,—the right of men to their own selves and to their liberties.

In solemn conclave our fathers had issued to the world that glorious manifesto, the Declaration of Independence. A little later, that the fundamental principles of liberty might have the best organization, they gave to this land our imperishable Constitution. Our flag means, then, all that our fathers meant in the Revolutionary War; all that the Declaration of Independence meant; it means all that the Constitution of our people, organizing for justice, for liberty, and for happiness, meant. Our flag carries American ideas, American history and American feelings. Beginning with the colonies, and coming down to our time, in its sacred heraldry, in its glorious insignia, it has gathered and stored chiefly this supreme idea: *Divine right of liberty in man*. Every color means liberty; every thread means liberty; every form of star and beam or stripe of light means liberty; not lawlessness, not license; but organized, institutional liberty,—liberty through law, and laws for liberty!

This American flag was the safeguard of liberty. Not an atom of crown was allowed to go into its insignia. Not a symbol of authority in the ruler was permitted to go into it. It was an ordinance of liberty by the people for the people. *That* it meant, *that* it means, and, by the blessing of God, *that* it shall mean to the end of time!

THE FLAG

James Jeffrey Roche

AN INCIDENT OF STRAIN'S EXPEDITION

I never have got the bearings quite,
   Though I've followed the course for many a year,
If he was crazy, clean outright,
   Or only what you might say was "queer."
He was just a simple sailor man.
   I mind it as well as yisterday,
When we messed aboard of the old Cyane.
   Lord! how the times does slip away!
That was five and thirty year ago,
   And I never expect such times again,
For sailors wasn't afraid to stow
   Themselves on a Yankee vessel then.
He was only a sort of bosun's mate,
   But every inch of him taut and trim;
Stars and anchors and togs of state
   Tailors don't build for the like of him.
He flew a no-account sort of name,
   A reg'lar fo'castle "Jim" or "Jack,"
With a plain "McGinnis" abaft the same,
   Giner'ly reefed to simple "Mack."
Mack, we allowed, was sorter queer,—
   Ballast or compass wasn't right.
Till he licked four Juicers one day, a fear
   Prevailed that he hadn't larned to fight.
But I reckon the Captain knowed his man,
   When he put the flag in his hand the day
That we went ashore from the old Cyane,
   On a madman's cruise for Darien Bay.

Forty days in the wilderness
   We toiled and suffered and starved with Strain,
Losing the number of many a mess
   In the Devil's swamps of the Spanish Main.

All of us starved, and many died.
   One laid down, in his dull despair;
His stronger messmate went to his side—
   We left them both in the jungle there.
It was hard to part with shipmates so;
   But standing by would have done no good.
We heard them moaning all day, so slow
   We dragged along through the weary wood.
McGinnis, he suffered the worst of all;
   Not that he ever piped his eye
Or wouldn't have answered to the call
   If they'd sounded it for "All hands to die."
I guess 't would have sounded for him before,
   But the grit inside of him kept him strong,
Till we met relief on the river shore;
   And we all broke down when it came along.

All but McGinnis. Gaunt and tall,
   Touching his hat, and standing square:
"Captain, the Flag."—And that was all;
   He just keeled over and foundered there.
"The Flag?" We thought he had lost his head—
   It mightn't be much to lose at best—
Till we came, by and by, to dig his bed,
   And we found it folded around his breast.
He laid so calm and smiling there,
   With the flag wrapped tight about his heart;
Maybe he saw his course all fair,
   Only—*we* couldn't read the chart.

WHAT AMERICA EXPECTS OF ITS YOUTH

Mrs. J. Borden Harriman

America is not perfect. My generation knows that. But it is ours, and it has been for a century the dream of freedom of every European. We must keep it so. Its streets have never been paved with gold, and they never will be, but I should like to think that even for the democracies in the north, we should stand as a land of opportunity and enthusiasm and riches. By riches I mean not only raw materials, armies, navies, railroads, ships and cities, but a whole people full of good will towards the world, loyal to its own flag and beautiful continent, ready to work to educate its whole people.

The ancient republic of Greece, the modern kingdom of Greece, the Ancient empire of China, the modern and war torn republic of Asia, the United States of America, see what we have in common. *That* is something every American young man should study.

To prepare yourselves for the times you live in you must look over the whole world to find your allies in building a world of equality of opportunity for all classes and all races, for the greater part of mankind will be happiest in a democratic society. But do not hope to have your democracy in far places, or worth fighting for elsewhere, if in your own house, own schools, own factories and shops, in your own country and city, you do not find the slogans and spirit and the daily practice of helping each other and keeping your eyes open to know and guard not only your own advantage, but the common interests of mankind in justice and peace. Remember to rejoice and be happy over your blessings. Hold fast to your ideals. Lift up your eyes to the hills and realize that "Where there is no vision, the people perish."

From THE MEANING OF THE FLAG

Woodrow Wilson

How can any man presume to interpret the emblem of the United States, the emblem of what we would fain be among the family of nations, and find it incumbent upon us to be in the daily round of routine duty? This is Flag Day, but that only means that it is a day when we are to recall the things which we should do every day of our lives. There are no days of special patriotism. There are no days when we should be more patriotic than on other days. We celebrate the Fourth of July merely because the great enterprise of liberty was started on the Fourth of July in America, but the great enterprise of liberty was not begun in America. It is illustrated by the blood of thousands of martyrs who lived and died before the great experiment on this side of the water. The Fourth of July merely marks the day when we consecrated ourselves as a nation to this high thing which we pretend to serve. The benefit of a day like this is merely in turning away from the things that distract us, turning away from the things that touch us personally and absorb our interest in the hours of daily work. We remind ourselves of those things that are greater than we are, of those principles by which we believe our hearts to be elevated, of the more difficult things that we must undertake in these days of perplexity when a man's judgment is safest only when it follows the line of principle.

I am solemnized in the presence of such a day. I would not undertake to speak your thoughts. You must interpret them for me. But I do feel that back, not only of every public official, but of every man and woman of the United States, there marches that great host which has brought us to the present day; the host that has never forgotten the vision which it saw at the birth of the nation; the host which always responds to the dictates of humanity and of liberty; the host that will always constitute the strength and the great body of friends of every man who does his duty to the United States.

I am sorry that you do not wear a little flag of the Union every day instead of some days. I can only ask you, if you lose the physical emblem, to be sure that you wear it in your heart, and the heart of America shall interpret the heart of the world.

THE NOBLEST PUBLIC VIRTUE

Henry Clay

There is a sort of courage, which, I frankly confess it, I do not possess,—a boldness to which I dare not aspire, a valour which I cannot covet. I cannot lay myself down in the way of the welfare and happiness of my country. That, I cannot—I have not the courage to do. I cannot interpose the power with which I may be invested—a power conferred, not for my personal benefit, nor for my aggrandisement, but for my country's good—to check her onward march to greatness and glory. I have not courage enough. I am too cowardly for that. I would not, I dare not, in the exercise of such a threat, lie down, and place my body across the path that leads my country to prosperity and happiness. This is a sort of courage widely different from that which a man may display in his private conduct and personal relations. Personal or private courage is totally distinct from that higher and nobler courage which prompts the patriot to offer himself a voluntary sacrifice to his country's good.

Apprehensions of the imputation of the want of firmness sometimes impel us to perform rash and inconsiderate acts. It is the greatest courage to be able to bear the imputation of the want of courage. But pride, vanity, egotism, so unamiable and offensive in private life, are vices which partake of the character of crimes, in the conduct of public affairs. The unfortunate victim of these passions cannot see beyond the little, petty, contemptible circle of his own personal interests. All his thoughts are withdrawn from his country, and concentrated on his consistency, his firmness, himself! The high, the exalted, the sublime emotions of a patriotism which, soaring towards Heaven, rises far above all mean, low, or selfish things, and is absorbed by one soul-transporting thought of the good and the glory of one's country, are never felt in his impenetrable bosom. That patriotism which, catching its inspiration from the immortal God, and, leaving at an immeasurable distance below all lesser, grovelling, personal interests and feelings, animates and prompts to deeds of self-sacrifice, of valour, of devotion, and of death itself,—that is public virtue; that is the noblest, the sublimest of all public virtues!

From THE MAN WITHOUT A COUNTRY

Edward Everett Hale

As we lay back in the stern sheets and the men gave way, he said to me: "Youngster, let that show you what it is to be without a family, without a home, and without a country. And if you are ever tempted to say a word or to do a thing that shall put a bar between you and your family, your home, and your country, pray God in his mercy to take you that instant home to his own heaven. Stick by your family, boy; forget you have a self, while you do everything for them. Think of your home, boy; write and send and talk about it. Let it be nearer and nearer to your thought the farther you have to travel from it; and rush back to it when you are free, as that poor black slave is doing now. And for your country, boy," and the words rattled in his throat, "and for that flag," and he pointed to the ship, "never dream a dream but of serving her as she bids you, though the service carry you through a thousand hells. No matter what happens to you, no matter who flatters you or who abuses you, never look at another flag, never let a night pass but you pray God to bless that flag. Remember, boy, that behind all these men you have to do with, behind officers, and Government, and people even, there is the Country Herself, your Country, and that you belong to Her as you belong to your own mother. Stand by Her, boy, as you would stand by your mother, if those devils there had got hold of her to-day!"

INDEPENDENCE DAY

James Gillespie Blaine

The United States is the only country with a known birthday. All the rest begun, they know not when, and grew into power, they know not how. If there had been no Independence Day, England and America combined would not be so great as each actually is. There is no "Republican," no "Democrat," on the Fourth of July,—all are Americans. All feel that their country is greater than party.

From PREFACE TO 1855 EDITION OF LEAVES OF GRASS

Walt Whitman

The Americans of all nations at any time upon the earth have probably the fullest poetical nature. The United States themselves are essentially the greatest poem. In the history of the earth hitherto the largest and most stirring appear tame and orderly to their ampler largeness and stir. Here at last is something in the doings of man that corresponds with the broadcast doings of the day and night. Here is not merely a nation but a teeming nation of nations. Here is action untied from strings necessarily blind to particulars and details magnificently moving in vast masses. Here is the hospitality which forever indicates heroes. . . . Here are the roughs and beards and space and ruggedness and nonchalance that the soul loves. Here the performance disdaining the trivial unapproached in the tremendous audacity of its crowds and groupings and the push of its perspective spreads with crampless and flowing breadth and showers its prolific and splendid extravagance. One sees it must indeed own the riches of the summer and winter, and need never be bankrupt while corn grows from the ground or the orchards drop apples or the bays contain fish or men beget children upon women.

Other states indicate themselves in their deputies . . . but the genius of the United States is not best or most in its executives or legislatures, nor in its ambassadors or authors or colleges or churches or parlors, nor even in its newspapers or inventors . . . but always most in the common people. Their manners speech dress friendships—the freshness and candor of their physiognomy—the picturesque looseness of their carriage . . . their deathless attachment to freedom—their aversion to anything indecorous or soft or mean—the practical acknowledgment of the citizens of one state by the citizens of all other states—the fierceness of their roused resentment—their curiosity and welcome of novelty—their self-esteem and wonderful sympathy—their susceptibility to a slight—the air they have of persons who never knew how it felt to stand in the presence of superiors—the fluency of their speech—their delight in music, the sure symptom of manly tenderness and native elegance of soul . . . their good temper and open-handedness—the terrible significance of their elections—the President's taking off his hat to them not they to him—these too are unrhymed poetry. It awaits the gigantic and generous treatment worthy of it.

THE GREAT MELTING POT

Israel Zangwill

"America is God's crucible, the Great Melting Pot, where all the races of Europe are reforming. Here you stand, goodfolk, think I, when I see them at Ellis Island, here you stand in your fifty groups with your fifty languages and histories and your fifty blood-hatreds and rivalries. But you won't long be like that, brothers, for these are the fires of God you've come to—these are the fires of God. A fig for your feuds and vendettas. Germans and Frenchmen, Irishmen and Englishmen, Jews and Russians, into the crucible with you all. God is making the American."

THE SPIRIT OF AMERICA

Woodrow Wilson

From CHICAGO SPEECH

America lives in the heart of every man everywhere who wishes to find a region where he will be free to work out his destiny as he chooses.

100th Year of Base ball

Norman Rockwell

LIBERTY TREE

Thomas Paine

1

In a chariot of light from the regions of day,
    The Goddess of Liberty came;
Ten thousand celestials directed the way,
    And hither conducted the dame.
A fair budding branch from the gardens above,
    Where millions with millions agree,
She brought in her hand, as a pledge of her love,
    And the plant she named, *Liberty tree*.

2

The celestial exotic struck deep in the ground,
    Like a native it flourish'd and bore.
The fame of its fruit drew the nations around,
    To seek out this peaceable shore.
Unmindful of names or distinctions they came,
    For freemen like brothers agree,
With one spirit endued, they one friendship pursued,
    And their temple was *Liberty tree*.

3

Beneath this fair tree, like the patriarchs of old,
    Their bread in contentment they eat,
Unvex'd with the troubles of silver and gold,
    The cares of the grand and the great.
With timber and tar they Old England supply'd,
    And supported her power on the sea;
Her battles they fought, without getting a groat,
    For the honour of *Liberty tree*.

4

But hear, O ye swains, ('tis a tale most profane),
    How all the tyrannical powers,
King, Commons, and Lords, are uniting amain,
    To cut down this guardian of ours;
From the east to the west, blow the trumpet to arms,
    Thro' the land let the sound of it flee,
Let the far and the near,—all unite with a cheer,
    In defence of our *Liberty tree*.

LIBERTY

Patrick Henry

Three millions of people, armed in the holy cause of *liberty*, and in such a country as we possess, are invincible by any force which our enemy can send against us. Besides, sir, we shall not fight our battle alone. There is a just God who presides over the destinies of nations, and who will raise up friends to fight our battles for us. The battle, sir, is not to the strong alone; it is for the vigilant, the active, the brave. Besides, sir, we have no election. If we were base enough to desire it, it is now too late to retire from the contest. There is no retreat but in submission and slavery! Our chains are forged! Their clanking may be heard on the plains of Boston! The war is inevitable—and let it come! I repeat, sir, let it come!

It is in vain, sir, to extenuate the matter. Gentlemen may cry, Peace, Peace—but there is no peace. The war is actually begun! The next gale that sweeps from the north will bring to our ears the clash of resounding arms! Our brethren are already in the field! Why stand we here idle? What is it that gentlemen wish? What would they have? Is life so dear, or peace so sweet, as to be purchased at the price of chains and slavery? Forbid it, Almighty God! I know not what course others may take; but as for me, give me *liberty* or give me death!

THREES

Carl Sandburg

I was a boy when I heard three red words
a thousand Frenchmen died in the street
for: Liberty, Equality, Fraternity—I asked
why men die for words.

I was older; men with mustaches, sideburns,
lilacs, told me the high golden words are:
Mother, Home, and Heaven—other older men with
face decorations said: God, Duty, Immortality
—they sang these threes slow from deep lungs.

Years ticked off their say-so on the great clocks
of doom and damnation, soup and nuts: meteors flashed
their say-so: and out of great Russia came three
dusky syllables workmen took guns and went out to die
for: Bread, Peace, Land.

And I met a marine of the U.S.A., a leatherneck with
a girl on his knee for a memory in ports circling the
earth and he said: Tell me how to say three things
and I always get by—gimme a plate of ham and eggs—
how much?—and—do you love me, kid?

COOL TOMBS

Carl Sandburg

When Abraham Lincoln was shoveled into the tombs, he forgot
    the copperheads and the assassin . . . in the dust, in the cool
    tombs.

And Ulysses Grant lost all thought of con men and Wall Street,
    cash and collateral turned ashes . . . in the dust, in the cool
    tombs.

Pocahontas' body, lovely as a poplar, sweet as a red haw in
    November or a pawpaw in May, did she wonder? does she
    remember? . . . in the dust, in the cool tombs?

Take any streetful of people buying clothes and groceries, cheer-
    ing a hero or throwing confetti and blowing tin horns . . . tell
    me if the lovers are losers . . . tell me if any get more than the
    lovers . . . in the dust . . . in the cool tombs.

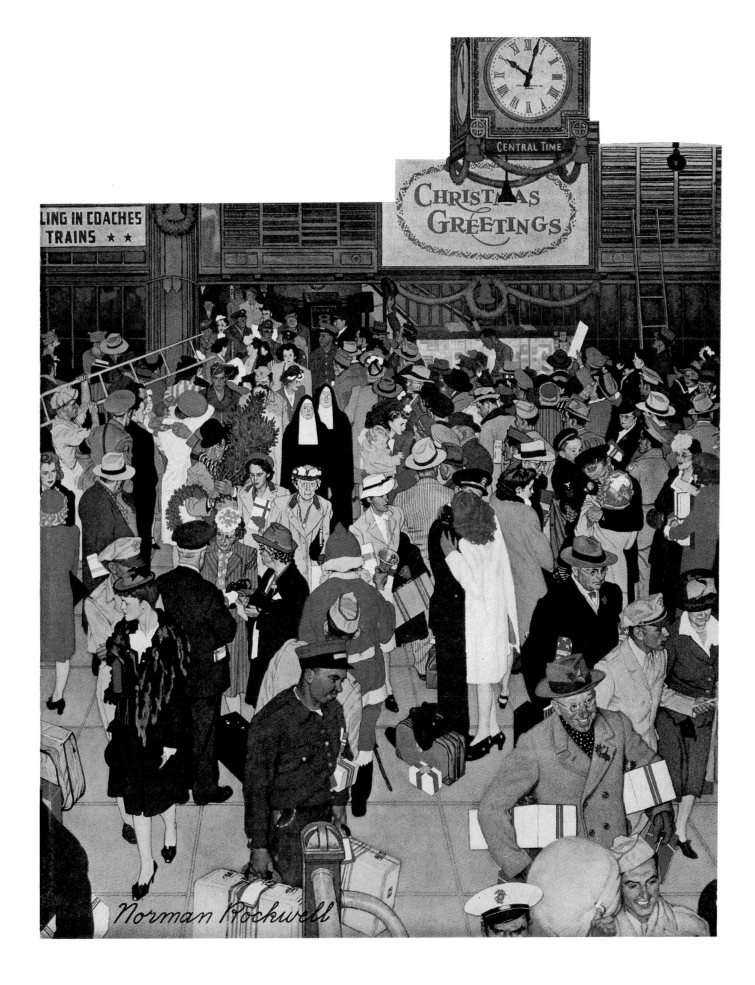

THE UNKNOWN CITIZEN

W. H. Auden

He was found by the Bureau of Statistics to be
One against whom there was no official complaint,
And all the reports on his conduct agree
That, in the modern sense of an old-fashioned word, he was a
　　　saint,
For in everything he did he served the Greater Community.
Except for the War till the day he retired
He worked in a factory and never got fired,
But satisfied his employers, Fudge Motors Inc.
Yet he wasn't a scab or odd in his views,
For his Union reports that he paid his dues,
(Our report on his Union shows it was sound)
And our Social Psychology workers found
That he was popular with his mates and liked a drink.
The Press are convinced that he bought a paper every day
And that his reactions to advertisements were normal in every
　　　way.
Policies taken out in his name prove that he was fully insured,
And his Health-card shows he was once in hospital but left it
　　　cured.
Both Producers Research and High-Grade Living declare
He was fully sensible to the advantages of the Installment Plan
And had everything necessary to the Modern Man,
A phonograph, a radio, a car and a frigidaire.
Our researchers into Public Opinion are content
That he held the proper opinions for the time of year;
When there was peace, he was for peace; when there was
　　　war, he went.
He was married and added five children to the population,
Which our Eugenist says was the right number for a parent
　　　of his generation,
And our teachers report that he never interfered with their
　　　education.
Was he free? Was he happy? The question is absurd:
Had anything been wrong, we should certainly have heard.

BRAVE NEW WORLD

Archibald MacLeish

But you, Thomas Jefferson
You could not lie so still,
You could not bear the weight of stone
On the quiet hill,

You could not keep your green grown peace
Nor hold your folded hand
If you could see your new world now,
Your new sweet land.

There was a time, Tom Jefferson,
When freedom made free men.
The new found earth and the new freed mind
Were brothers then.

There was a time when tyrants feared
The new world of the free.
Now freedom is afraid and shrieks
At tyranny.

Words have not changed their sense so soon
Nor tyranny grown new.
The truths you held, Tom Jefferson,
Will still hold true.

What's changed is freedom in this age.
What great men dared to choose
Small men now dare neither win
Nor lose.

Freedom, when men fear freedom's use
But love its useful name,
Has cause and cause enough for fear
And cause for shame.

We fought a war in freedom's name
And won it in our own.

We fought to free a world and raised
A wall of stone.

Your countrymen who could have built
The hill fires of the free
To set the dry world all ablaze
With liberty—

To burn the brutal thorn in Spain
Of bigotry and hate
And the dead lie and the brittle weed
Beyond the Plate.

Who could have heaped the bloody straw,
The dung of time, to light
The Danube in a sudden flame
Of hope by night—

Your countrymen who could have hurled
Their freedom like a brand
Have cupped it to a candle spark
In a frightened hand.

Freedom that was a thing to use
They've made a thing to save
And staked it in and fenced it round
Like a dead man's grave.

You, Thomas Jefferson,
You could not lie so still,
You could not bear the weight of stone
On your green hill,

You could not hold your angry tongue
If you could see how bold
The old stale bitter world plays new
And the new world old.

From TRAVELS WITH CHARLEY

John Steinbeck

It would be pleasant to be able to say of my travels with Charley, "I went out to find the truth about my country and I found it." And then it would be such a simple matter to set down my findings and lean back comfortably with a fine sense of having discovered truths and taught them to my readers. I wish it were that easy. But what I carried in my head and deeper in my perceptions was a barrel of worms. I discovered long ago in collecting and classifying marine animals that what I found was closely intermeshed with how I felt at the moment. External reality has a way of being not so external after all.

This monster of a land, this mightiest of nations, this spawn of the future, turns out to be the macrocosm of microcosm me. If an Englishman or a Frenchman or an Italian should travel my route, see what I saw, hear what I heard, their stored pictures would be not only different from mine but equally different from one another. If other Americans reading this account should feel it true, that agreement would only mean that we are alike in our Americanness.

From start to finish I found no strangers. If I had, I might be able to report them more objectively. But these are my people and this my country. If I found matters to criticize and to deplore, they were tendencies equally present in myself. If I were to prepare one immaculately inspected generality it would be this: For all of our enormous geographic range, for all of our sectionalism, for all of our interwoven breeds drawn from every part of the ethnic world, we are a nation, a new breed. Americans are much more American than they are Northerners, Southerners, Westerners, or Easterners. And descendants of English, Irish, Italian, Jewish, German, Polish are essentially American. This is not patriotic whoop-de-do; it is carefully observed fact. California Chinese, Boston Irish, Wisconsin German, yes, and Alabama Negroes, have more in common than they have apart. And this is the more remarkable because it has happened so quickly. It is a fact that Americans from all sections and of all racial extractions are more alike than the Welsh are like the English, the Lancashireman like the Cockney, or for that matter the Lowland Scot like the Highlander. It is astonishing that this has happened in less than two hundred years and most of it in the last fifty. The American identity is an exact and provable thing.

Starting on my return journey, I realized by now that I could not see everything. My impressionable gelatin plate was getting muddled. I determined to inspect two more sections and then call it a day—Texas and a sampling of the Deep South. From my reading, it seemed to me that Texas is emerging as a separate force and that the South is in the pain of labor with the nature of its future child still unknown. And I have thought that such is the bitterness of the labor that the child has been forgotten.

This journey had been like a full dinner of many courses, set before a starving man. At first he tries to eat all of everything, but as the meal progresses he finds he must forgo some things to keep his appetite and his taste buds functioning.

I bucketed Rocinante out of California by the shortest possible route—one I knew well from the old days of the 1930s. From Salinas to Los Banos, through Fresno and Bakersfield, then over the pass and into the Mojave Desert, a burned and burning desert even this late in the year, its hills like piles of black cinders in the distance, and the rutted floor sucked dry by the hungry sun. It's easy enough now, on the high-speed road in a dependable and comfortable car, with stopping places for shade and every service station vaunting its refrigeration. But I can remember when we came to it with prayer, listening for trouble in our laboring old motors, drawing a plume of steam from our boiling radiators. Then the broken-down wreck by the side of the road was in real trouble unless someone stopped to offer help. And I have never crossed it without sharing something with those early families foot-dragging through this terrestrial hell, leaving the white skeletons of horses and cattle which still mark the way.

The Mojave is a big desert and a frightening one. It's as though nature tested a man for endurance and con-

stancy to prove whether he was good enough to get to California. The shimmering dry heat made visions of water on the flat plain. And even when you drive at high speed, the hills that mark the boundaries recede before you. Charley, always a dog for water, panted asthmatically, jarring his whole body with the effort, and a good eight inches of his tongue hung out flat as a leaf and dripping. I pulled off the road into a small gulley to give him water from my thirty-gallon tank. But before I let him drink I poured water all over him and on my hair and shoulders and shirt. The air is so dry that evaporation makes you feel suddenly cold.

I opened a can of beer from my refrigerator and sat well inside the shade of Rocinante, looking out at the sun-pounded plain, dotted here and there with clumps of sagebrush.

About fifty yards away two coyotes stood watching me, their tawny coats blending with sand and sun. I knew that with any quick or suspicious movement of mine they could drift into invisibility. With the most casual slowness I reached down my new rifle from its sling over my bed—the .222 with its bitter little high-speed, long-range stings. Very slowly I brought the rifle up. Perhaps in the shade of my house I was half hidden by the blinding light outside. The little rifle has a beautiful telescope sight with a wide field. The coyotes had not moved.

I got both of them in the field of my telescope, and the glass brought them very close. Their tongues lolled out so that they seemed to smile mockingly. They were favored animals, not starved, but well furred, the golden hair tempered with black guard hairs. Their little lemon-yellow eyes were plainly visible in the glass. I moved the cross hairs to the breast of the right-hand animal, and pushed the safety. My elbows on the table steadied the gun. The cross hairs lay unmoving on the brisket. And then the coyote sat down like a dog and its right paw came up to scratch the right shoulder.

My finger was reluctant to touch the trigger. I must be getting very old and my ancient conditioning worn thin. Coyotes were vermin. They steal chickens. They thin the ranks of quail and all other game birds. They must be killed. They are the enemy. My first shot would drop the sitting beast, and the other would whirl to fade away. I might very well pull him down with a running shot because I am a good rifleman.

And I did not fire. My training said, "Shoot!" and my age replied, "There isn't a chicken within thirty miles, and if there are any they aren't my chickens. And this waterless place is not quail country. No, these boys are keeping their figures with kangaroo rats and jackrabbits, and that's vermin eat vermin. Why should I interfere?"

"Kill them," my training said. "Everyone kills them. It's a public service." My finger moved to the trigger. The cross was steady on the breast just below the panting tongue. I could imagine the splash and jar of angry steel, the leap and struggle until the torn heart failed, and then, not too long later, the shadow of a buzzard, and another. By that time I would be long gone—out of the desert and across the Colorado River. And beside the sagebrush there would be a naked, eyeless skull, a few picked bones, a spot of black dried blood and a few rags of golden fur.

I guess I'm too old and too lazy to be a good citizen. The second coyote stood sidewise to my rifle. I moved the cross hairs to his shoulder and held steady. There was no question of missing with that rifle at that range. I owned both animals. Their lives were mine. I put the safety on and laid the rifle on the table. Without the telescope they were not so intimately close. The hot blast of light tousled the air to shimmering.

Then I remembered something I heard long ago that I hope is true. It was unwritten law in China, so my informant told me, that when one man saved another's life he became responsible for that life to the end of its existance. For, having interfered with a course of events, the savior could not escape his responsibility. And that has always made good sense to me.

Now I had a token responsibility for two live and healthy coyotes. In the delicate world of relationships, we are tied together for all time. I opened two cans of dog food and left them as a votive.

I have driven through the Southwest many times, and even more often have flown over it—a great and mysterious wasteland, a sun-punished place. It is a mystery, something concealed and waiting. It seems deserted, free of parasitic man, but this is not entirely so. Follow the double line of wheel tracks through sand and rock and you will find a habitation somewhere huddled in a protected place, with a few trees pointing their roots at under-earth water, a patch of starveling corn and squash, and strips of jerky hanging on a string. There is a breed of desert men, not hiding exactly but gone to sanctuary from the sins of confusion.

At night in this waterless air the stars come down just out of reach of your fingers. In such a place lived the hermits of the early church piercing to infinity with un-littered minds. The great concepts of oneness and of majestic order seem always to be born in the desert. The quiet counting of the stars, and observation of their movements, came first from desert places. I have known desert men who chose their places with quiet and slow passion, rejecting the nervousness of a watered world. These men have not changed with the exploding times except to die and be replaced by others like them.

And always there are mysteries in the desert, stories told and retold of secret places in the desert mountains where surviving clans from an older era wait to re-emerge. Usually these groups guard treasures hidden from the waves of conquest, the golden artifacts of an archaic Montezuma, or a mine so rich that its discovery would change the world. If a stranger discovers their existence, he is killed or so absorbed that he is never seen again. These stories have an inevitable pattern untroubled by the question, If none return, how is it known what is there? Oh, it's there all right, but if you find it you will never be found.

And there is another monolithic tale which never changes. Two prospectors in partnership discover a mine of preternatural richness—of gold or diamonds or rubies. They load themselves with samples, as much as they can carry, and they mark the place in their minds by landmarks all around. Then, on the way out to the other world, one dies of thirst and exhaustion, but the other crawls on, discarding most of the treasure he has grown too weak to carry. He comes at last to a settlement, or perhaps is found by other prospecting men. They examine his samples with great excitement. Sometimes in the story the survivor dies after leaving directions with his rescuers, or again he is nursed back to strength. Then a well-equipped party sets out to find the treasure, and it can never be found again. That is the invariable end of the story—it is never found again. I have heard this story many times, and it never changes. There is nourishment in the desert for myth, but myth must somewhere have its roots in reality.

And there are true secrets in the desert. In the war of sun and dryness against living things, life has its secrets of survival. Life, no matter on what level, must be moist or it will disappear. I find most interesting the conspiracy of life in the desert to circumvent the death rays of the all-conquering sun. The beaten earth appears defeated and dead, but it only appears so. A vast and inventive organization of living matter survives by seeming to have lost. The gray and dusty sage wears oily armor to protect its inward small moistness. Some plants engorge themselves with water in the rare rainfall and store it for future use. Animal life wears a hard, dry skin or an outer skeleton to defy the desiccation. And every living thing has developed techniques for finding or creating shade. Small reptiles and rodents burrow or slide below the surface or cling to the shaded side of an outcropping. Movement is slow to preserve energy, and it is a rare animal which can or will defy the sun for long. A rattlesnake will die in an hour of full sun. Some insects of bolder inventiveness have devised personal refrigeration systems. Those animals which must drink moisture get it at second hand—a rabbit from a leaf, a coyote from the blood of a rabbit.

One may look in vain for living creatures in the daytime, but when the sun goes and the night gives consent, a world of creatures awakens and takes up its intricate pattern. Then the hunted come out and the hunters, and hunters of the hunters. The night awakes to buzzing and to cries and barks.

When, very late in the history of our planet, the incredible accident of life occurred, a balance of chemical factors, combined with temperature, in quantities and in kinds so delicate as to be unlikely, all came together in the retort of time and a new thing emerged, soft and helpless and unprotected in the savage world of unlife. Then processes of change and variation took place in the organisms, so that one kind became different from all others. But one ingredient, perhaps the most important of all, is planted in every life form—the factor of survival. No living thing is without it, nor could life exist without this magic formula. Of course, each form developed its own machinery for survival, and some failed and disappeared while others peopled the earth. The first life might easily have been snuffed out and the accident may never have happened again—but, once it existed, its first quality, its duty, preoccupation, direction, and end, shared by every living thing, is to go on living. And so it does and so it will until some other accident cancels it. And the desert, the dry and sun-lashed desert, is a good school in which to observe the cleverness and the infinite variety of techniques of survival under pitiless opposition. Life could not change the sun or water the desert, so it changed itself.

The desert, being an unwanted place, might well be the last stand of life against unlife. For in the rich and moist and wanted areas of the world, life pyramids against itself and in its confusion has finally allied itself with the enemy non-life. And what the scorching, searing, freezing, poisoning weapons of non-life have failed to do may be accomplished to the end of its destruction and extinction by the tactics of survival gone sour. If the most versatile of living forms, the human, now fights for survival as it always has, it can eliminate not only itself but all other life. And if that should transpire, unwanted places like the desert might be the harsh mother of re-population. For the inhabitants of the desert are well trained and well armed against desolation. Even our own misguided species might reemerge from the desert. The lone man and his sun-toughened wife who cling to the shade in an unfruitful and uncoveted place might, with their brothers in arms—the coyote, the jackrabbit, the horned toad, the rattlesnake, together with a host of armored insects—these trained and tested fragments of life might well be the last hope of life against non-life. The desert has mothered magic things before this.

From LAID BACK IN WASHINGTON

Art Buchwald

GOD DOESN'T VOTE

God is really getting a workout during this election year. There was a time when the TV preachers devoted their programs to telling us how angry God was with the way we were behaving in our private lives, which of course is their business.

But now we're being told that God has a vested interest in whom we put into public office, and some Fundamentalist sects, known as the Moral Majority, are spending wads of money to defeat anybody whose voting record doesn't go along with their interpretation of the Bible.

They are calling for a holy war against those who are for the ERA, pro-abortion, school busing and are against the B-1 bomber.

I always thought the nice thing about God was that he stayed out of American politics.

But after watching the TV shows for the past few weeks, I was beginning to wonder.

So when I spoke to God the other night I asked, "Whom are you going to vote for this year?"

God seemed very angry. "I never take sides in an American election."

"But there are a lot of people down here who say you want Reagan."

"That's ridiculous. I hardly know the man, though I have seen his movies."

"But the Bible thumpers keep quoting you all the time. They say you've definitely made your mind up and we'd better all go along with you or we're headed for damnation."

"With all due respect to these people, they don't know what the devil they're talking about. I've told them time and time again that I don't give political endorsements. If I did, I wouldn't be God. I have a good mind to sue them for using my name without my permission."

"I don't blame you," I said. "And I for one never believed them when they kept quoting you on the political issues."

"What scares me," God said, "is that these TV ministers are not only telling the American people whom I support, but they're raising all their money in my name. They keep warning the viewing audience that if they don't send in their checks, I'm going to be very upset. I don't deal in money—never have and never will. But they're telling those poor souls out there that if they don't come up with a contribution, they won't have any salvation. I'd appreciate it if you put the word out that anyone is free to send in any amount of money to a TV minister, but the money isn't buying them a place in heaven. It's buying limousines and private airplanes and $500 suits for the people who are making the pitches."

"God, you sound mad."

"I *am* mad. I'm trying to keep the whole world from blowing up and those preachers down there say my only concern is to defeat George McGovern in South Dakota."

"I wish you could somehow get the message over that you aren't for or against anyone running in our elections this year. It would certainly clear the air for all of us."

"I can't do it. I believe in the separation of church and state. I've stayed out of American politics since 1776 and that's why you people are still around. I'm sorry. I have to go now, I have the Moral Majority on hold."

THE BOYS ON THE BUS

"The Boys on the Bus" is the title given to newspaper people who travel with presidential candidates. The phrase was made famous by Tim Crouse in his excellent book concerning the McGovern-Nixon campaign.

At the beginning of this year's presidential race, there were quite a few buses to choose from. The top political writers and TV commentators had first choice of which bus they wanted to take. Everyone wanted to get on John Connally's bus because it looked as if he had the best chance of beating Reagan for the Republican nomination. George Bush's bus was half empty before Iowa, as was Howard Baker's. Bob Dole had a mini-bus, and if you wanted to follow Anderson around, you could always get a ride with him in his Volkswagen.

On the Democratic side, there was a serious bus problem when Teddy Kennedy got into the race. The pundits had predicted that as soon as he challenged Carter, the nomination would be his for the asking. So all the media stars fought to get on Teddy's bus.

WHY ARE PEOPLE MUMBLING?

It may be my imagination, but more and more people seem to be talking to themselves during this election year. All you have to do is walk down the street and you can hear someone mumbling. I was curious to hear what people are saying, so I followed one man who was muttering. This is what I heard:

"I can't vote for Carter—anyone but Carter. . . . But then I can't vote for Reagan either. . . . If I go for Anderson, I'll be throwing my vote away. . . . I better vote for Carter. But Carter doesn't seem to know what he's doing. He got us into a recession, and in four more years, he could get us into a depression. . . . I better vote for Reagan. . . . Reagan will get us into a war. It would be terrible to be in a recession and a war at the same time. . . . I better vote for Anderson. . . . What do I know about Anderson? I voted for Carter last time because I didn't know anything about him. I won't make that mistake again. . . . I better vote for Carter. . . .

"I'm not sure I could stand the Georgia Mafia for another four years. I better vote for Reagan. . . . But if I vote for Reagan, I'll be voting for simple answers to complicated questions. He hasn't said anything original since *Bedtime for Bonzo*. . . . Maybe I better vote for Anderson. Why should I vote for Anderson? He seems honest—but they all seem honest at the beginning. I'll bet underneath it all, he's just another politician on the make. . . . I think I'll cast my ballot for Carter. What am I saying? The reason I'm having all this trouble deciding who to vote for is because of Carter. He hasn't solved any of the problems we're facing. . . . He says one thing one day and another the next. . . . It looks as if I have no choice. I have to pull the lever for Reagan. . . . But if Reagan gets in, he may have two or three Supreme

Court appointments. I couldn't live with the people Reagan would appoint to the Supreme Court.

"It's obvious. I have to forget the two-party system and support Anderson. . . . Hold it. . . . Anderson can't win. All he can do is spoil it for the other two and then it will go to the House, and they'll probably give it to Carter. I might as well vote for Carter in the first place. . . . My wife said she'd never talk to me if I voted for Carter again. She says she's had it with Born-Again Presidents. . . . I don't think Reagan's been born again. I wonder if she'd want me to vote for Reagan? . . . I wish she hadn't left home to take a job in California so I could ask her. . . . I guess it has to be Reagan. . . . No, it doesn't have to be Reagan. He never gets his facts straight. That's all right when you're running for office—but it could be real trouble in the Oval Office. . . . I better think Anderson. . . . Anderson? Is he just a media star who will burn out once the election is over? . . . Where did he come from? What do I know about him except he looked different from the others? . . . I have to come to my senses. I'm not happy about it, but I'll go for Carter.

"But if I vote for Carter, we'll get the whole damn family in the White House again. . . . I'm not sure I can put up with Amy in her teens, and I know I've had it with Billy. At least with Reagan we don't get a family. . . . It's obvious what my decision is. I'll vote for Reagan and take my chances. Some people say he was a good governor of California. Come to think of it, he's the one who said it. Others say he fudged his record. . . . Maybe I should vote for Anderson and forget about the whole thing. But Anderson's record in the House isn't all that hot either. He says he's changed his mind on a lot of things. . . . Well, if he can change his mind, so can I. At least I know what I'm getting with Carter. If anyone asks me, I'm a Carter man. . . . I can't say it with a straight face. Can I say I'm a Reagan man with a straight face? Nope, I can't do that either. I can say I'm an Anderson man with a straight face. Look at my straight face. It isn't straight? I was afraid of that.

"So where does that leave me? Maybe Carter has learned a lot in the first four years and will be a good President in his second term? It's happened before. When did it happen? How do I know? . . . If I vote for Reagan, he said he'll only stay for one term. . . . That's

158

SO YOU WANT TO SEE THE PRESIDENT!

By NORMAN ROCKWELL

THE SATURDAY EVENING POST
FOUNDED IN 1728 BY Benj. Franklin

Photographers waiting outside Executive Wing entrance for a newsworthy face. Your credentials are checked again behind that door by Secret Service.

"Credentials, please," says MP at White House gate.

During a lull, White House reporters catch up on their newspaper reading and a Nelson Rockefeller man (*left*) waits to see the President.

Lull breaks sharply when word comes that Presidential Secretary Steve Early has some news to release, and reporters flock down a corridor to Early's office.

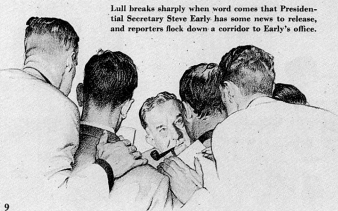

SOMETIMES it seems to the busy White House staff as if everybody on this good green hemisphere wants to see the President of the United States personally. With a small segment of our population this is a chronic disease; with most Americans it is simply an expression of honest curiosity and interest. It was with this understandable interest in mind that White House authorities recently permitted Post Artist Norman Rockwell to roam the Executive Wing and make a visual report on what the process of getting in to see the President is like. As the drawings and paintings show, Rockwell found the Wing a fascinating antechamber of democracy, and he says he couldn't imagine such an atmosphere of dignified informality prevailing just outside the sanctum of a dictator or king. The waiting facilities are comfortable and easy on the eye. The secretarial staff is cheerful and courteous; so are the omnipresent Secret Service men, who manage to protect the President from possible harm with Gestapo-like efficiency, but without shoving anyone around. Conversation among the callers is subdued in tone, but uninhibited. The White House newspaper correspondents go about freely, buttonholing heroes, legislators, beauty-contest winners and ambassadors, and doing their own invaluable job of keeping America in touch with its main listening post. The atmosphere is, on the whole, neighborly and friendly. Your trip through the anteroom of The Boss, as the staff speaks of him, awaits you in these pages. —*The Editors.*

9

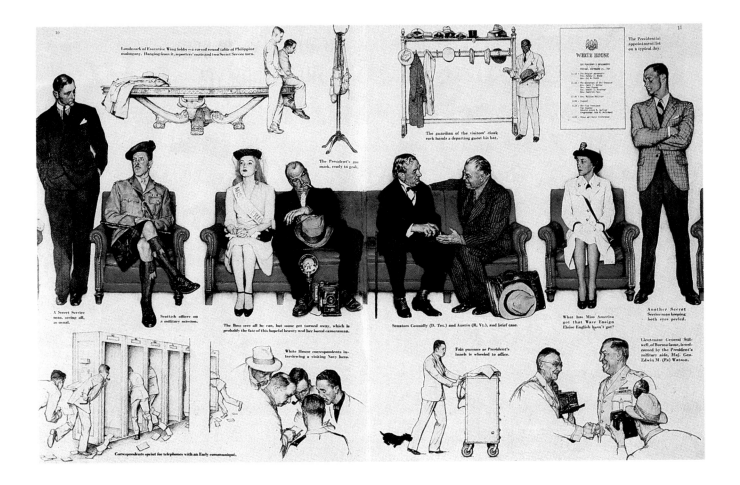

in his favor. But then again I have to consider his age. Of course, his hair is dark. Anderson's is white. I wonder why Anderson's hair is white. . . . Can the country survive with a white-haired President?

"There has to be a solution to my problem. . . . Wait a minute. I think I have it. Why didn't I think of it before? I'll move to Chicago and vote for all three."

THE THRILL IS GONE

"Let's have an early dinner and then watch the election results," I said to my wife Tuesday night.

"That's a good idea," she agreed. "It's going to be a long evening but we'll get a head start."

We finished dinner at 8:15 P.M. and then went into the living room to sit back and watch what the pollsters had predicted would be one of the closest elections in history. I flipped on the set and heard either Tom Brokaw or John Chancellor announce: "NBC has projected that Ronald Reagan has won the election and will be the next President of the United States."

"What the hell is going on?" I asked my wife. "I haven't even finished my yogurt yet."

"Look at the map. The Eastern part of it is all blue."

"It takes Archie Bunker longer to open a door than it does to decide a presidential election," I said.

"How do they know?" my wife asked.

"I think they use an exit poll. They ask a black man in Buffalo, a Jewish man in Virginia, a housewife in Florida, a med student in Ohio and a steelworker in Pennsylvania whom they voted for, and then they start making the map all blue for Reagan. Would you care to play a game of Scrabble?"

"If we had known what was going to happen," my wife said, "we could have had an early dinner after the election results.

"I can't believe it," she said. "The polls aren't even closed in three-quarters of the states."

Since I had nothing to do, I called my friend Bernheim in California. I got him at his office.

"Where are you going tonight to watch the election results?"

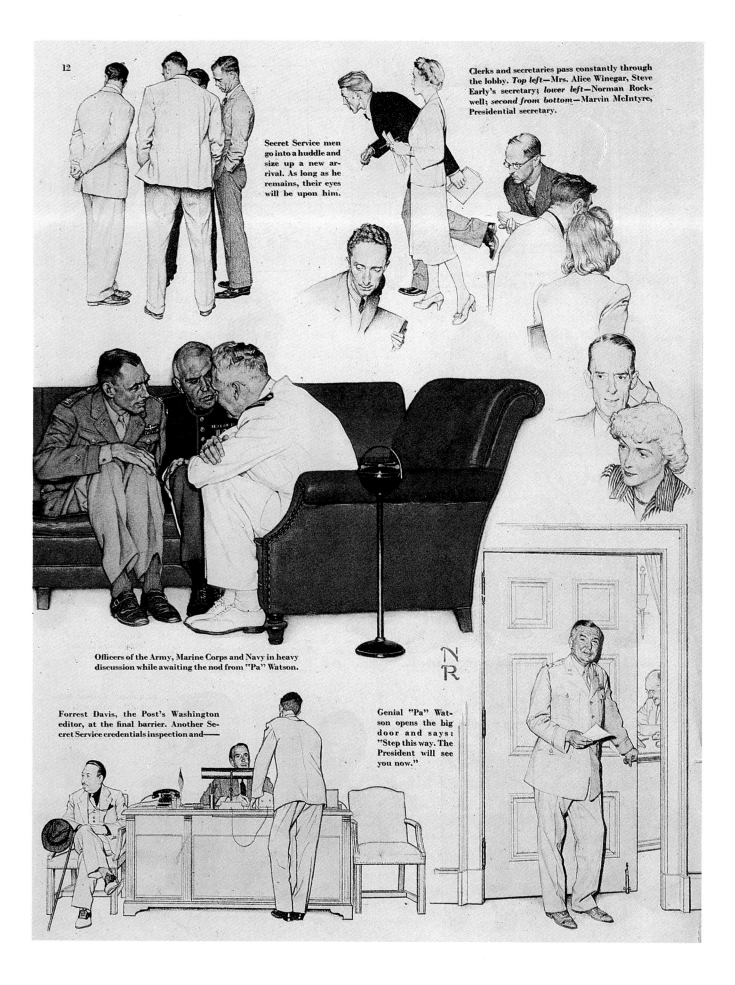

Secret Service men go into a huddle and size up a new arrival. As long as he remains, their eyes will be upon him.

Clerks and secretaries pass constantly through the lobby. *Top left*—Mrs. Alice Winegar, Steve Early's secretary; *lower left*—Norman Rockwell; *second from bottom*—Marvin McIntyre, Presidential secretary.

Officers of the Army, Marine Corps and Navy in heavy discussion while awaiting the nod from "Pa" Watson.

Forrest Davis, the Post's Washington editor, at the final barrier. Another Secret Service credentials inspection and——

Genial "Pa" Watson opens the big door and says: "Step this way. The President will see you now."

"To Phyllis and Don's," he said. "I have to go home and get cleaned up first, and then vote."

"I wouldn't do that if I were you, Alain."

"Why not?"

"Reagan won, and there isn't a thing anyone in California can do about it."

"What do you mean, he won? It's only 4:15 P.M. here. How could he have won?"

"He took Ohio, Michigan, New Jersey, Connecticut and Illinois."

"Where did you hear this?"

"It's all over television. NBC interviewed a senior citizen in Delaware and then gave the election to Reagan. Do you know what this means, Alain?"

"I'm not sure."

"The network polling methods have become so sophisticated we don't need anyone west of the Mississippi to decide a presidential election anymore. You people are only wasting the nation's gasoline by going to the polls."

"But we're the most populous state in the union," Bernheim protested.

"Don't tell me your troubles. It's all over, Alain. As I talk to you, Barbara Walters is trying to get Nancy Reagan, and Walter Cronkite has just said, 'And that's the way it is November 4th, 1980.' Do you need any more evidence that you people are out of it?"

"Then you think I shouldn't vote?"

"Why not? It will kill some time when you get home. But if you think you're going to stop the landslide, you're out of your gourd."

"I guess I'll call Phyllis and Don. Maybe they can cancel the caterer. Where's Ann?"

"She went to bed with a headache. She said she's not going to spend any more election nights with me. As far as our political life is concerned, she claims the thrill is gone."

From BLUE HIGHWAYS

William Least Heat Moon

Nobody was sure about the figures around here. According to one waterman, of the hundreds of skipjacks once dredging oysters from Chesapeake Bay, about a dozen remained at Tilghman Island and perhaps an equal number at Deal Island; another man thought there might be as many as forty on the entire bay. Two men said skipjacks were doomed, but another held that expensive fuel would bring them back. He believed the old ships, with refinements, would become the new ships and that the diesel boats replacing the skipjacks were the temporary ones.

Even though no new skipjacks had been built since 1956, the aging fleet still survived by virtue of a Maryland law, designed to prevent overharvesting, that allows dredging under motor power only on Mondays and Tuesdays. One other thing made for the survival of that single-masted, double-sailed boat of low and majestic lines. People here, now that the bugeyes are gone, consider the skipjack the very symbol of the Eastern Shore. It is to them what the beanpot is to a Bostonian.

I went north, crossed Chesapeake Bay, and stopped at the city market down among the eighteenth-century streets of Annapolis to eat a dozen fresh clams at Hannon's stone counter; for the road I bought a cut of smoked chub, a quart of slaw, and six bottles of Black Horse Ale. I took Maryland 2 over the hills along the bay, turned west on Prince Frederick, crossed the wide Patuxent River, on through Burnt Store and Allen's Fresh, across the even wider Potomac. I came into Virginia on state 218, an old route now almost forgotten. The towns, typically, were a general store and a few dispersed houses around a crossroads: Osso, Goby, Passapatanzy.

In Fredericksburg (home of George Washington's brother-in-law, Colonel Fielding Lewis, a cannon manufacturer whom the Episcopalians buried in an honored position under the steps of Saint George's Church—*salve lucrum!*), I stopped at a U-pump gas station—one of those places where you push your credit card through a slot to the on-duty commandant of the fuel islands. I asked for the air hose. "Ain't got no air," he said. I might as well have gone to a fireplug for service. The age of self-serve.

I suffered a reflex of nostalgia: back in the age of inner tubes, Vernon's Service actually sold gasoline *and* service. Vern wore a little black plastic clip-on bowtie and stub-billed cap that gave him the look of a smudged motorcycle cop; with a faded red wiping rag hanging from his hip pocket, Vern over the years made an oily trail between the pumps and grease pit. He washed windshields with real sponges that he ran through a little wringer kept by the ethyl pump: I think his wife laundered them twice a week. But the men's restroom wasn't any cleaner than now, and there wasn't a hot water faucet then either; but you didn't need a key to get in, and his mother wouldn't let him install quarter machines vending latex health aids.

There were only two posted rules at Vernon's (one an old gas station apothegm): WE AIM TO PLEASE, YOU AIM TOO PLEASE. The other, NO TOOLS LOANED, was necessary because people liked Vern and actually asked to borrow his tools. Tools: Vern had no diagnostic equipment other than a good ear and eye, and he could correct a surprising assortment of problems with a screwdriver and adjustable wrench.

Even then, Vern was an anachronism. We boys who collected at his station didn't call him that, of course. We called him, as I remember, "an old fart." Vern, in his antique ways, believed that anyone who got behind a steering wheel could rightly be issued an *Operator's* Permit. He believed the more work a driver did, the less the car had to do; the less it had to do, the simpler and more reliable and cheaper to repair it would be. He cursed the increasing complexity of automobile mechanics. But, as I say, he was a man of the old ways. He even believed in narrow tires (cheaper and less friction), spoked wheels (less weight), and the streamlined "Airflow" designs of Chrysler Corporation cars of the mid-thirties—designs Chrysler almost immediately gave up on before proceeding to build the biggest finned hogs of all. We boys of the fifties loved their brontosaurean bulk.

Another of Vernon's themes we laughed at was his advocacy of the comparable economy and safety of three-wheels (he drove a motorcycle with a sidecar) for city driving. He would say to us. "Two wheels ain't enough, and four's too many. So where does that leave you, boys?" "Three wheels!" we'd shout back, mocking him. "No sir, it leaves money in your jeans."

So much for antiquity.

I went down to Civil War Spotsylvania for the night. The heavy fighting for control of the important crossroads in front of the Spotsylvania County Courthouse occurred in fields and woods a couple of miles away, and now the intersection linked the bluest of back roads, a crossing of so little economic, logistic, and strategic importance as to make the conflict between Lee and Grant appear imbecilic. The big battlefield outside town is today a national historic site marking the series of battles that began at a place called "the Wilderness."

Atop one hill, with forest behind and open land in front, at a little bend in the breastworks, troops fought what may have been the longest and most savage hand-to-hand combat of the war: the Battle of Bloody Angle. The fighting here in the wet spring of 1864 was so close that cannoneers, standing ankle deep in mud, fired at point-blank range; soldiers, slogging it out in a smoky rainstorm, fought muzzle to muzzle, stabbing with bayonets, thrusting swords between logs of the parapet, clubbing each other into the mire from dawn to midnight, and trampling fallen men out of sight into the muck. The intense rifle fire cut in half oak trees two feet in diameter. One soldier, Horace Porter, wrote: "We had not only shot down an army, but also a forest."

On that single day of May 12, nearly thirteen thousand men died fighting over one square mile of ground abandoned by both sides several days later. Yet, had anyone been paying attention, the battle could have shown the futility of trench warfare, a lesson that would have to be learned again at even higher cost in the First World War.

At that "bivouac of the dead," as one monument had it, I ate the smoked chub. Across the grassy meadow stood a shaft commemorating the Ohio contingent; among the carved names: Gashem Arnold, Elam Dye, Lewis Wolf, Enos Swinehart.

Three children raced from under the oaks out over the grass to reenact the battle with guttural gunshots from their boyish throats. They argued briefly about who would be who: one chose the Americans, one the Germans, one the Irish. The small cries of the boys, and the bugs chirring out the last of spring, and the warmth of the evening sun almost turned Bloody Angle to an idyllic meadow. But its history was the difference. Even though Titans and Tridents and MX's have not made "the red business," as Whitman called it, a thing of the past, they have eliminated future battlefield parks where boys can play at war—unless scientists find means to hang monuments in the sky.

2

Captain Jack Jouett probably didn't have a chance against the fame of Paul Revere, yet Jouett's deed was comparable: on June 4, 1781, Captain Jack rode his bay mare, Sallie, forty miles from Cuckoo Tavern to Charlottesville to warn Thomas Jefferson, Patrick Henry, and that nest of sedition, the Virginia General Assembly, that Bloody Tarleton's Green Dragons were coming. Jouett rode without stopping, while the British raiders stopped three times—once to burn a wagontrain—and thereby lost both the rebels' capture and a chance at dramatic incident. A good thing for American history. And for Henry Wadsworth Longfellow. Jouett is a devilish name to rhyme.

When I saw Cuckoo, Virginia, it was a historical marker and a few houses at an intersection. I went up U.S. 33 until the rumple of hills became a long, bluish wall across the western sky. On the other side of

Stanardsville in the Blue Ridge Mountains, I stopped in a glen and hiked along Swift Run, a fine rill of whirligigs and shiners, until I found a cool place for lunch. Summer was a few days away, but the heat wasn't.

Water striders and riffle bugs cut angles and arcs on smooth backwaters of the stream that reflected cirrus clouds crossing the ridges. They would make West Virginia before I did. I was sitting at the bottom of the eastern side of the Appalachians; when I came out of the mountains again, I would be in the Middlewest. Sixteen dollars in my pocket. The journey was ending.

In a season on the blue roads, what had I accomplished? I hadn't sailed the Atlantic in a washtub, or crossed the Gobi by goat cart, or bicycled to Cape Horn. In my own country, I had gone out, had met, had shared. I had stood as witness.

I took a taste of Swift Run, went back to the highway, and followed it up Massanutten Mountain. Again the going was winding and slow. Near sunset, I reached West Virginia and drove on to Franklin, a main-street hamlet sharing a valley with a small river as the Appalachian towns do. Above the South Fork, above a hayfield, and under the mountains, I pulled in for the night.

After a small meal in the Ghost, I marked on a map the wandering circle of my journey. From the heartland out and around. A blue circle gone beyond itself. "Everything the Power of the World does is done in a circle," Black Elk says. "Even the seasons form a great circle in their changing, and always come back again to where they were. The life of a man is a circle from childhood to childhood, and so it is in everything where power moves."

Then I saw a design. There on the map, crudely, was the labyrinth of migration the old Hopis once cut in their desert stone. For me, the migration had been to places and moments of glimpsed clarity. Splendid gifts all.

3

The state seal of West Virginia is not a used tire hanging on a fencepost any more than the state flag is a tattered cloth used as an automobile gas tank cap. But well it could be. Heaped in yards, sliding down hills, hanging from trees and signs were old tires. It seemed as if West Virginia sat at the bottom of a mountain where Americans came annually to throw away their two hundred million used tires.

Along highway 33 lay hardscrabble farms, as the thirties called them, of rocky fields, dwindly crops, houses partly painted in two or three colors, trumpet vine crawling iron bedstead trellises, and jimson weed taking warped five-rail fences (kiss the middle rail to cure chapped lips). In the few places large and level enough for true fields, men were putting up hay by hand.

The road, a thing to wrench an eel's spine, went at the mountains in all the ways: up, down, around, over, through, under, between. I've heard—who knows the truth?—that if you rolled West Virginia out like a flapjack, it would be as large as Texas. Where possible in the mountainous interruptions, towns opened briefly: Judy Gap, Mouth of Seneca, Elkins.

At Buckhannon, I drove southwest on state 4. Beautiful country despite hills clobbered with broken appliances and automobile fragments, which children turned into Jungle gyms. Should you ever go looking for some of the six hundred million tons of ferrous scrap rusting away in America, start with West Virginia.

Then Sutton, hidden in the slant of mountains at the heart of the state, a town that began in 1805 when John O'Brien took up residence in a hollow sycamore along the Elk River. Now Sutton was an old place of grizzled and maimed men who could have been the last survivors of the Union Army; one missing a right hand, one the left, another with a patched eye, one minus a nose, one an ear; as for limps and bent spines, I couldn't count them all. And the teeth! Broken, rotted, snaggled, bucked, splintered. An orthodontist's paradise. But that wasn't what struck me about Sutton. What struck me was the similarity in the faces, as though a man's father were his brother and his uncle his first cousin. A town of more kin than kith. Sutton, I think, may be the place where those people you see waiting in bus stations for the 1:30 A.M. express are going.

In the frayed, cluttery hamlet everything—people, streets, buildings—seemed to be nearing an end. In one old survivor, Elliott's Fountain (CIGARS CANDY SUNDRIES around the window, Ex-Lax thermometer by the tall door, YOUR WATE AND FATE scale there also, and inside a ceramic tile floor in the pattern of a diamondback rattler). I drank a Hamilton-Beach chocolate milkshake, the kind served alongside the stainless steel mixing cup.

The owner, Hugh Elliott, laid out a 1910 photograph of the drugstore when you could buy a freshly concocted purge or balm, or a fountain Bromo-Seltzer, or a dulcimer; although the pharmaceuticals were gone, you could still get a Bromo or a dulcimer (next to the Texas Instruments 1025 Memory Calculator). The photograph showed one other change: what had been a spacious room of several bent-steel chairs and tables was now top to bottom with merchandise. What had been a place of community was now a stuffed retail outlet. Across the nation, that change was the history of the soda fountain pharmacy.

A crisp little lavender-and-lace lady, wearing her expansion-band wristwatch almost to the elbow to keep it in place, sipped a cherry phosphate and pointed out in the photograph the table where her husband—dead these twenty years—had proposed to her. She said, "You won't find me at the grave. Always feel closer to him in here with a phosphate."

When I drove out of Sutton, clouds moved in and the heavy sky sagged with drizzle. It was part of the sixty inches of yearly rainfall here. I fought it a few miles, then gave up and stopped in the old railroad town of Gassaway at the Elk Lunch, formerly the Farmers and Merchants Bank. Handpainted vertically down the worn Doric granite columns: LUNCH BEER. I had one of each.

Next to me a man, whose stomach started at his neck and stopped below his groin, said, "Ain't from around here, I see."

"How's that?"

"Wiped that beer bottle off fore you swigged on it."

As I ate my hamburger, the fellow explained the best means of taking a catfish. During the long explanation rivaling Izaak Walton's for detail, the man periodically formed a funnel with his index finger and thumb and poured salt into his bottle of Falls City. "Used to could taste the beer in our country," he said. The angling method was this: first "bait" a catfish hole with alfalfa and pork fat for three weeks; then, the night before a rain, put a nine-lived Everready in a sealed Mason jar and lower it into the water to hang just in front of the baited hook.

PIONEER

Norman
Rockwell

"And it works well?" I asked.

"It works sometimes."

When I left, the day had turned to mist, and a red grit came off the highway and glazed the windshield. Like looking through a great bloodshot eye. State 4 followed the Elk River, an occluded green thickness that might have been split pea purée. The Elk provided a narrow bench, the only level land, and on it people had built homes, although the river lay between them and the road and necessitated hundreds of little handmade bridges— many of them suspension footbridges, the emblem of Appalachia. From rock ledges broken open by the highway cut, where seeps dripped, hung five-gallon galvanized buckets to collect the spring water.

Again came the feeling I'd had all morning, that somehow I'd made a turn in time rather than in space and driven into the thirties. The only things that showed a later decade were the pickup trucks: clean and new, unlike the rattling, broken automobiles.

West Virginia 36, a quirk of a road, went into even more remote land, the highway so narrow my right tires repeatedly dropped off the pavement. Towns: Valleyfork, Wallback, and Left Hand (a school, church, post office, and large hole once the Exxon station). west lay the Pennzoil country of small valleys barbed with rusting derricks, the great flywheels turning slowly, inexorably like the mills of God that grind exceeding fine.

I hunched over the steering wheel as if to peer under the clouds, to see beyond. I couldn't shake the sense I was driving in another era. Maybe it was the place or maybe a slow turning in the mind about how a man cannot entirely disconnect from the past. To try to is the American impulse, but to look at the steady continuance of the past is to watch time get emptied of its bluster because time bears down less on the continuum than on the components. To be only a nub in the eternal temporary is still to have a chance to see, a chance to pry at the mystery. What is the blue road anyway but an opportunity to poke at the unseen and a hoping the unseen will poke back?

At Spencer, I turned west onto U.S. 33. The Appalachians flattened themselves to hills, and barnsides again gave the Midwest imperative: CHEW MAIL POUCH. With what was left of day, I crossed the Ohio River into old Gallipolis, a town of a dozen pronunciations, a gazebo-on-the-square town settled by eighteenth-century Frenchmen. Although a priest once placed a curse on Gallipolis—I don't know why—residents today claim it's the loveliest French village on the Ohio.

4

"Inquire Locally," the road should have been marked. Of the thirteen thousand miles of highway I'd driven in the last months, Ohio 218 through Gallia County set a standard to measure bad road by with pavement so rough I looked forward to sections where the blacktop was gone completely. Along the shoulders lay stripped cars, presumably from drivers who had given up. Yet the sunny county was a fine piece of washed grasses, gleams in hounds' eyes, constructions of spiders, rocks broken and rounded—all those things and fully more.

At Ironton I took the river road down a stretch of power lines, rail lines, water lines, and telephone lines (the birds sleep across the water on the wooded Kentucky bluffs, they say). The old riverbank towns—Franklin Furnace, New Boston, Portsmouth, Friendship, Manchester, Utopia—now found the Ohio more a menace than a means of livelihood, and they had shifted northward to string out along the highway like kinks in a hawser. I had no mind for stopping. God's speed, people once wished the traveler.

At Cincinnati, I looped the city fast on the interstate and came to Indiana 56, where corn, tobacco, and bluesailor grew to the knee, and also wild carrot, fleabane, golden Alexander. Apples were coming into a high green, butterflies stitched across the road, and all the way the whip of mowers filled Ghost Dancing sweetly with the waft of cut grass. Each town had its feed and grain store, each farm its grain bin and corncrib. Rolling, rolling, the land, the road, the truck.

I dropped south to New Harmony, Indiana, twelve miles downstream from Grayville, Illinois, where I'd spent that first grim night. New Harmony in June piles up with the sprinkle from golden rain trees, here called "gate trees." The town is known for two experiments in social engineering, both of which failed. Yet those failures put in motion currents that changed the course of what came after: the abolition of slavery, equal opportunity for women, progressive education, emancipation from poverty. The futuristic village was once even the headquarters for the U.S. Geologic Survey.

Rappites from Pennsylvania created the town of Harmonie out of bosky Wabash River bottomland in 1814. They grew wheat, vegetables, grapes, apples, and hops; they produced wine, woolens, tinware, shoes, and whiskey. The Rappite Golden Rose trademark, like the Shaker name, became an assurance of quality. A decade later, however, as the struggle of primitive life eased, members began finding more time for reflection; to blunt a growing discontent, the leader, George Rapp, sold the village to Robert Owen and moved the colony back to Pennsylvania, where the people could again start from scratch and live the peace of full occupation. Seventy-five years later, their Shaker-like refusal to have any truck with the future brought about their disappearance.

Owen, the British industrialist, utopian, and egalitarian, who worked to create a society free of ignorance and selfishness by eliminating the "causes of contest among individuals" (his basic tenet was "circumstances form character"), renamed the town New Harmony and built a cooperative community that developed into a center for creative social and scientific thought in antebellum America. Yet, before the first settler died, egotism and greed did the experiment in. New Harmony survived, but only as a monument to idealism and innovation.

Not far from a burial ground of unmarked graves that the old Harmonists share with a millennium of Indians, the mystical Rappites in 1820 planted a circular privet-hedge labyrinth, "symbolic" (a sign said) "of the Harmonist concept of the devious and difficult approach to a state of true harmony." After the Rappites, the hedges disappeared, but a generation ago, citizens replanted the maze, its contours strikingly like the Hopi map of emergence. I walked through it to stretch from the long highway. Even though I avoided the shortcut holes broken in the hedges, I still went down the runs and curves without a single wrong turn. The "right" way was worn so deeply in the earth as to be unmistakable. But without the errors, wrong turns, and blind alleys, without the doubling back and misdirection and fumbling and chance discoveries, there was not one bit of joy in walking the labyrinth. And worse: knowing the way made traveling it perfectly meaningless.

Before I crossed the Wabash (Algonquian for "white shining"), I filled the gas tank—enough for the last leg. From the station I could see the blue highway curving golden into the western afternoon. I'd make Columbia by nightfall.

The circle almost complete, the truck ran the road like the old horse that knows the way. If the circle had come full turn, I hadn't. I can't say, over the miles, that I had learned what I had wanted to know because I hadn't known what I wanted to know. But I *did* learn what I didn't know I wanted to know.

The highway before, under, behind. Through the Green-River-ordinance-enforced towns. Past barnlot windmills that said AERMOTOR CHICAGO. On and on. The Mississippi River. Then the oak risings of Missouri.

The pump attendant, looking at my license plate when he had filled the tank, asked, "Where you coming from, Show Me?"

"Where I've been."

"Where else?" he said.

THE OUTLOOK

287 FOURTH AVENUE

NEW YORK

OFFICE OF

THEODORE ROOSEVELT

28 May, 1912

Friend William:

Your letter contains really the philosophy of my canvass. After all, I am merely standing for the principles which you and I used to discuss so often in the old days both in the Maine woods and along the Little Missouri. They are the principles of real Americans and I believe that more and more the plain people of the country are waking up to the fact that they are the right principles. I look forward to seeing you soon.

Faithfully yours,

T. Roosevelt

W. W. Sewall, Esq.
    Island Falls, Maine

MARE LIBERUM

Henry van Dyke

You dare to say with perjured lips,
   "We fight to make the ocean free?"
You, whose black trail of butchered ships
   Bestrews the bed of every sea
Where Germans submarines have wrought
Their horrors! Have you never thought,—
   What you call freedom, men call piracy!

Unnumbered ghosts that haunt the wave
   Where you have murdered, cry you down;
And seamen whom you would not save
   Weave now in weed-grown depths a crown
Of shame for your imperious head,—
A dark memorial of the dead,—
   Women and children whom you sent to drown.

Nay, not till thieves are set to guard
   The gold, and corsairs called to keep
O'er peaceful commerce watch and ward,
   And wolves to herd the helpless sheep,
Shall men and women look to thee,
Thou ruthless Old Man of the Sea,
   To safeguard law and freedom on the deep!

In nobler breeds we put our trust:
   The nations in whose sacred lore
The "Ought" stands out above the "Must,"
   And honor rules in peace and war.
With these we hold in soul and heart,
With these we choose our lot and part,
   Till liberty is safe on sea and shore.

From ONLY IN AMERICA

Harry Golden

THIS COULD HAPPEN ONLY IN AMERICA

I need a book; a book that may be found only in the Library of Congress, or maybe in the Library of Harvard University. And so I call up the Charlotte Public Library, and ask for either Mr. Galvin or Mr. Brockman. I tell him what I want and where I think it may be found and within a week or ten days the book or the document is delivered to me on a two-week loan. I can renew it if I give them a few days' prior notice, and thus the facilities provided by my city in the South are expanded through cooperation with the facilities and treasures of the whole of America, and merely for the asking. They all combine to make available to me the sum total of all of human thought and experience; at no cost whatever.

A DAY WITH CARL SANDBURG

I spent eight hours with Carl Sandburg.

Except for a short walk around his Connemara Farm at Flat Rock, North Carolina, we sat on his porch and exchanged stories. But mostly we laughed just as the poet Blake imagined it— ". . . we laughed and the hills echoed."

Carl Sandburg and I spent eight hours together, and the sapphire mountains of North Carolina cast echo and shadow of Lincoln, of Swedish immigrant farmers to the broad plains of the American Midwest, of pushcarts on the Lower East Side of New York, and of a long-ago place in the province of Galicia in Austrian Poland— and this could happen only in America.

And when we rested from our labors, Margaret, the charming daughter of the Sandburgs, read to us out of George Ade, a household favorite.

Nor did even the dinner bell intrude upon us. "Bring it out here on the porch," said Mr. Sandburg; and I reflected later, with considerable chagrin, how I had not offered to help Mrs. Sandburg and Miss Margaret when they lugged the side tables to us; and they tried hard not to disturb us.

And when it was all over, Sandburg said, "Harry, it's been about fifty-fifty, you talked half and I talked half."

I am certain that Carl Sandburg had thought of this appointment as just another interview. Just another newspaper fellow, standing first on one foot and then on the other, asking how do I like North Carolina; what am I writing now; a question maybe about Lincoln, or Nancy Hanks, or Mary Todd; who is my favorite novelist; what do I think of *Andersonville*, etc.

I shuddered at the thought that he might associate me with such nonsense.

Nor did I carry a book for him to autograph, or a camera to snap his picture, or a manuscript for him to read in his "spare time." All I brought was a bottle of whiskey.

Whiskey? Who ever heard of bringing a bottle of whiskey to Carl Sandburg? Well, I figured that, even if he doesn't drink, he probably would not think it in bad taste if I drank a few toasts to him—right on the spot. Margaret Sandburg kept us supplied with fresh North Carolina branch water.

I had planned the appointment for a long time. Several years ago Don Shoemaker, the Asheville *Citizen-Times* editor, had introduced Mr. Sandburg to *The Carolina Israelite* and we exchanged a few letters during the past five years. Several months ago I wrote him for an appointment, and received a note:

> Brudder Golden: All signs say I'll be here April 3 and if you're here we won't expect to save the country but we can have fellowship. Carl Sandburg.

I arrived about noon and as I got out of the car I heard Sandburg's voice through the screen door of his porch: "That must be Harry Golden; I want to see what he looks like." There are about ten steps leading up to the porch of the old plantation home and when I reached the top Mr. Sandburg was already outside to greet me. He

SPRINGTIME

wore a Korean army cap low over his eyes, khaki shirt and work pants. I turned from him to take a long look at that breathtaking scene, the acres and acres of lawn as clean as a golf course in front of the house, the heavily wooded areas to the right, the majestic North Carolina Rockies in front—the whole thing like a Christmas card without snow, and I greeted Sandburg with the first thought that came into my head: "Well, I wonder what old Victor Berger would have said if he had seen this place." (Victor Berger, the first Socialist ever elected to Congress, was publisher of the Socialist paper *The Leader* on which Sandburg had worked in his early newspaper days.) Sandburg threw his head back and roared; called back into the house to Mrs. Sandburg. "He wants to know what Victor Berger would have said if he had seen this place," but then he motioned me to a chair on the porch and began to apologize in all seriousness for a proletariat's ownership of an old Southern plantation. "When did I get this place—1945, right? And how old was I in 1945—seventy years old, right?" But I told him he had nothing to worry about; that from some parapet in heaven Victor Berger and Eugene V. Debs look down upon Carl Sandburg with love and devotion and by now even the writer of Psalms has memorized a bit of Carl Sandburg:

> There is only one man in the world
> And his name is All Men.

We discussed socialism, of course, the American Socialist movement and the tragedy of so many, many uneducated editorial writers who speak of "Communism, socialism, etc." as though they were the same; and this, the supreme irony: wherever the Communists have conquered, the Socialists, the Social Democrats were *always* the first ones they killed. We spoke of the days when the movement was at its height, when Walter Lippmann was secretary to Socialist Mayor George Lunn of Schenectady, New York; and the party stalwarts included Margaret Sanger, Heywood Broun, Morris Hillquit, Algernon Lee, Alan Benson, August Claessens, and Charles P. Steinmetz, the electrical wizard.

We swapped tales of the Lower East Side of New York, the *Jewish Daily Forward*, and Morris Hillquit, who, foreign accent and all, was one of the best orators I

ever heard. And Sandburg brought out a volume of his poetry, *Smoke and Steel*, and read to me of the East Side:

HOME FIRES

In a Yiddish eating place on Rivington Street . . .
    faces . . . coffee spots . . . children kicking at the
    night stars with bare toes from bare buttocks.
They know it is September on Rivington Street
    when the red tomaytoes cram the pushcarts,
Here the children snozzle at milk bottles, children
    who have never seen a cow.
Here the stranger wonders how so many people
    remember
    where they keep home fires.

We talked of the poor immigrants and how much more it cost them to live than the rich. They bought a scuttle of coal for ten cents; a bushel was a quarter. This in the days of five-dollars-a-ton coal, and they were paying thirty-five dollars a ton in dribs and drabs the way poor people have to buy. I told about how the Germans paid no attention to bare floors, concentrating on overstuffed beds; but that the Irish were nuts about carpets and curtains even if they had no other furniture; and how the Jews paid little attention to either carpets or beds, and concentrated their all on *food* on the table, the carry-over from centuries in the ghetto and the will to survive, to survive at all costs.

Sandburg brought me a little volume by the late August Claessens, *Didn't We Have Fun!* Claessens was one of the most famous Socialists on the East Side, a man with a brilliant mind and a wonderful sense of humor. This little book is a humorous record of thirty years on a soapbox. Mr. Sandburg inscribed the book: "For Harry Golden, whose heart is not alien to agitators." Interesting, I had once carried the American Flag for August Claessens at one of his street-corner meetings.

This charming Claessens had represented his all-Jewish district in the New York Legislature and eventually joined the Arbeiter Ring (Workman's Circle). A Roman Catholic, Claessens said that he joined the Jewish fraternity because of its cemetery benefits: "The last place in this world the devil will look for a Gentile is in a Jewish Cemetery."

And, of course, Sandburg and I exchanged anecdotes about Emanuel Haldeman-Julius, the Little Blue Book fellow. Haldeman-Julius was a feature writer on Victor Berger's Socialist paper at the same time that Sandburg was a reporter. Later, Haldeman-Julius went to California, Sandburg went to the Chicago *News*, and thereafter wrote his CHICAGO, "Hog Butcher for the World," which started him on his way into the mind and heart of America.

We swapped a dozen stories about this interesting Emanuel who published and sold three hundred million books in his lifetime and was the father of America's paperback book industry. Emanuel would watch the sales of his Little Blue Books carefully. If a book sold fewer than 10,000 a year he gave it one more chance. For instance, Gautier's *Fleece of Gold* sold less than 10,000. The following year he changed the title to *The Quest of a Blonde Mistress*, exactly the type of story it is. Sales jumped up to 80,000

Late in the afternoon a car drove up with Florida license plates and Mr. Sandburg went down the porch steps to greet the visitor. I followed a step or two behind. The fellow wanted to know something about Lincoln's money policy. Mr. Sandburg was gracious in his greeting, but told the visitor, "It's all in my books; look in the index." An hour later a phone call for Mr. Sandburg, and through the open window I heard: "It's all in my books; look in the index." And after another phone call: "That was Senator Johnston of South Carolina; his daughter is writing a term paper on me and wants to come out. I told him to call me some time after May fifth."

We discussed Oscar Ameringer, Herbert Hoover, Richard Nixon, Clarence Darrow and the famous trial of the McNamaras, and Mr. Sandburg had a few new facts about Darrow's trouble with labor after the Los Angeles tragedy.

I was happy when he agreed that Anzia Yezierska and Abe Cahan were among the best "Jewish" writers of modern American literature. We discussed Chapel Hill and Sandburg told me that he has known Phillips Russell for over forty years. I told him that a literary columnist had included his name among a list of North Carolina Writers, and how someone disputed it as a bit of provincialism. Sandburg was indignant. "I pay my taxes here; and I shall die here; *indeed I am a North Carolina writer.*" He was genuinely sorry that he had not met Jimmie Street after I had told him all about the late novelist. "He was over here in Asheville, speaking one night, and if I had known about him then, I would have gone over." Street was a much greater writer than his books indicated, and we discussed how completely true that has been of others; and, of course, how it happens in reverse, too.

When Margaret Sandburg excused herself, she shook my hand with the best goodbye I have ever heard—"I wish we had put this day on a tape recorder. I would love to have had a playback of your conversation with my father."

But it was hard to break away, and finally after the second goodbye, Sandburg brought me another book, *Home Front Memo*, being a hundred or more newspaper columns Mr. Sandburg had written during the America First and phony war period. And Mr. Sandburg inscribed this book, too: "For Harry Golden, who is also slightly leftish, and out of jail, and loves the Family of Man."

At home the next day I thumbed through the volume and came across a paragraph in which Mr. Sandburg describes a parting with a close friend and how he had put his arms around him and kissed him on both cheeks: "the second time in my life I have done this."

I closed the book. I did not need to read any more for a little while. I recalled how the night before, as I was leaving, Carl Sandburg had put his arms around me and kissed me on both cheeks.

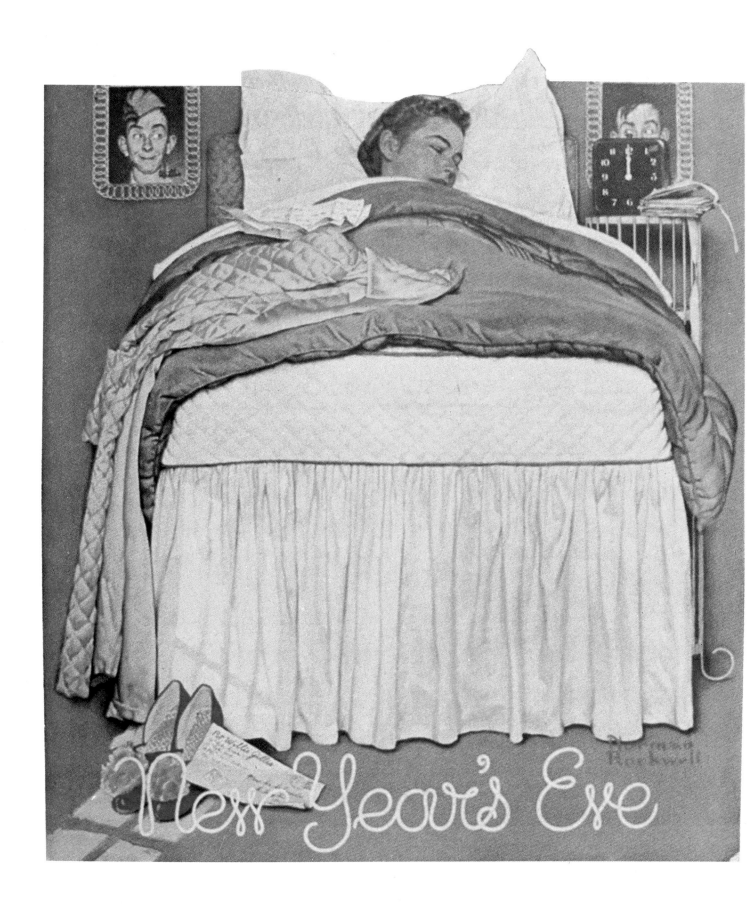

DREAMS

Langston Hughes

Hold fast to dreams
For if dreams die
Life is a broken-winged bird
That cannot fly.

Hold fast to dreams
For when dreams go
Life is a barren field
Frozen with snow.

ABRAHAM LINCOLN, 1809–1865

Stephen Vincent Benét

Lincoln was a long man.
He liked out of doors.
He liked the wind blowing
And the talk in country stores.

He liked telling stories,
He liked telling jokes.
"Abe's quite a character,"
Said quite a lot of folks.

Lots of folks in Springfield
Saw him every day,
Walking down the street
In his gaunt, long way.

Shawl around his shoulders,
Letters in his hat.
"That's Abe Lincoln."
They thought no more than that.

Knew that he was honest,
Guessed that he was odd,
Knew he had a cross wife
Though she was a Todd.

Knew he had three little boys
Who liked to shout and play,
Knew he had a lot of debts
It took him years to pay.

Knew his clothes and knew his house.
"That's his office, here.
Blame good lawyer, on the whole,
Though he's sort of queer.

"Sure, he went to Congress, once,
But he didn't stay.
Can't expect us all to be
Smart as Henry Clay.

"Need a man for troubled times?
Well, I guess we do.
Wonder who we'll ever find?
Yes—I wonder who."

That is how they met and talked,
Knowing and unknowing.
Lincoln was the green pine.
Lincoln kept on growing.

RACES

From A LETTER TO PRESIDENT
RICHARD M. NIXON FROM ROSALIND
FRANKLIN, AGE 11

Races are the colors of people's skin. Well, the kind I'm talking about.

Races are many different colors, red, white, brown and yellow.

I think races should stay together. Some people think differently, but I think we should stay together. As rainbow power. Colors put together.

Do you like how I put in the saying "rainbow power"?

THE HUNTER I MIGHT HAVE BEEN

George Mendoza

When I was a boy,
barely tall,
I shot a sparrow from a tree.
I held its limp body in my hands
and buried it still warm in the soft
earth.
Then I fled.
I never touched a gun again.
But years came later when I was
a man
I wondered,
oh, the hunter I might have been
had I but met a lion that first day
and not stilled that gentle
sparrow's call.

MR. LINCOLN'S WHISKERS

Burke Davis

Oct. 15, 1860

Hon A B Lincoln
Dear Sir

My father has just [come] home from the fair and brought home your picture and Mr. Hamlin's. I am a little girl only eleven years old, but want you should be President of the United States very much so I hope you wont think me very bold to write such a great man as you are. Have you any little girls about as large as I am if so give them my love and tell her to write to me if you cannot answer this letter. I have got 4 brother's and part of them will vote for you anyway and if you will let your whiskers grow I will try and get the rest of them to vote for you you would look a great deal better for your face is so thin. All the ladies like whiskers and they would tease their husband's to vote for you and then you would be President. My father is going to vote for you and if I was a man I would vote for you to but I will try and get every one to vote for you that I can. I think that rail fence around your picture makes it look very pretty I have got a little baby sister she is nine weeks old and just as cunning as can be. When you direct your letter dir[e]ct to Grace Bedell Westfield Chataque County New York

I must not write any more
answer this letter right off

Good bye
Grace Bedell

PRIVATE

Miss. Grace Bedell

Springfield, Ills.
Oct 19, 1860

My dear little Miss.

Your very agreeable letter of the 15th, is received.

I regret the necessity of saying I have no daughters. I have three sons—one seventeen, one nine, and one seven, years of age. They, with their mother, constitute my whole family.

As to the whiskers, having never worn any, do you not think people would call it a piece of silly affectation if I were to begin it now?

Your very sincere well-wisher
A. Lincoln

From THE RIGHT STUFF

Tom Wolfe

What an extraordinary grim stretch that had been . . . and yet thereafter Pete and Jane would keep running into pilots from other Navy bases, from the Air Force, from the Marines, who had been through their own extraordinary grim stretches. There was an Air Force pilot named Mike Collins. Mike Collins had undergone eleven weeks of combat training at Nellis Air Force Base, near Las Vegas, and in that eleven weeks twenty-two of his fellow trainees had died in accidents, which was an extraordinary rate of two per week. Then there was a test pilot, Bill Bridgeman. In 1952, when Bridgeman was flying at Edwards Air Force Base, sixty-two Air Force pilots died in the course of thirty-six weeks of training, an extraordinary rate of 1.7 per week. Those figures were for fighter-pilot trainees only; they did not include the test pilots, Bridgeman's own confreres, who were dying quite regularly enough.

Extraordinary, to be sure; except that every veteran of flying small high-performance jets seemed to have experienced these bad strings.

In time, the Navy would compile statistics showing that for a career Navy pilot, i.e., one who intended to keep flying for twenty years as Conrad did, there was a 23 percent probability that he would die in an aircraft accident. This did not even include combat deaths, since the military did not classify death in combat as accidental. Furthermore, there was a better than even chance, a 56 percent probability, to be exact, that at some point a career Navy pilot would have to eject from his aircraft and attempt to come down by parachute. In the era of jet fighters, ejection meant being exploded out of the cockpit by a nitroglycerine charge, like a human cannonball. The ejection itself was so hazardous—men lost knees, arms, and their lives on the rim of the cockpit or had the skin torn off their faces when they hit the "wall" of air outside—that many pilots chose to wrestle their aircraft to the ground rather than try it . . . and died that way instead.

The statistics were not secret, but neither were they widely known, having been eased into print rather obliquely in a medical journal. No pilot, and certainly no pilot's wife, had any need of the statistics in order to know the truth, however. The funerals took care of that in the most dramatic way possible. Sometimes, when the young wife of a fighter pilot would have a little reunion with the girls she went to school with, an odd fact would dawn on her: *they* have not been going to funerals. And then Jane Conrad would look at Pete . . . Princeton, Class of 1953 . . . Pete had already worn his great dark sepulchral bridge coat more than most boys of the Class of '53 had worn their tuxedos. How many of those happy young men had buried more than a dozen friends, comrades, and co-workers? (Lost through violent death in the execution of everyday duties.) At the time, the 1950's, students from Princeton took great pride in going into what they considered highly competitive, aggressive pursuits, jobs on Wall Street, on Madison Avenue, and at magazines such as *Time* and *Newsweek*. There was much fashionably brutish talk of what "dog-eat-dog" and "cutthroat" competition they found there; but in the rare instances when one of these young men died on the job, it was likely to be from choking on a chunk of Chateaubriand, while otherwise blissfully boiled, in an expense-account restaurant in Manhattan. How many would have gone to work, or stayed at work, on cutthroat Madison Avenue if there had been a 23 percent chance, nearly one chance in four, of dying from it? Gentlemen, we're having this little problem with chronic violent death . . .

And yet was there any basic way in which Pete (or Wally Schirra or Jim Lovell or any of the rest of them) was different from other college boys his age? There didn't seem to be, other than his love of flying. Pete's father was a Philadelphia stockbroker who in Pete's earliest years had a house in the Main Line suburbs, a limousine, and a chauffeur. The Depression eliminated the terrific brokerage business, the house, the car, and the servants; and by and by his parents were divorced and his father moved to Florida. Perhaps because his father had been an observation balloonist in the First World

War—an adventurous business, since the balloons were prized targets of enemy aircraft—Pete was fascinated by flying. He went to Princeton on the Holloway Plan, a scholarship program left over from the Second World War in which a student trained with midshipmen from the Naval Academy during the summers and graduated with a commission in the Regular Navy. So Pete graduated, received his commission, married Jane, and headed off to Pensacola, Florida, for flight training.

Then came the difference, looking back on it.

A young man might go into military flight training believing that he was entering some sort of technical school in which he was simply going to acquire a certain set of skills. Instead, he found himself all at once enclosed in a fraternity. And in this fraternity, even though it was military, men were not rated by their outward rank as ensigns, lieutenants, commanders, or whatever. No, herein the world was divided into those who had it and those who did not. This quality, this *it*, was never named, however, nor was it talked about in any way.

As to just what this ineffable quality was . . . well, it obviously involved bravery. But it was not bravery in the simple sense of being willing to risk your life. The idea seemed to be that any fool could do that, if that was all that was required, just as any fool could throw away his life in the process. No, the idea here (in the all-enclosing fraternity) seemed to be that a man should have the ability to go up in a hurtling piece of machinery and put his hide on the line and then have the moxie, the reflexes, the experience, the coolness, to pull it back in the last yawning moment—and then to go up again *the next day*, and the next day, and every next day, even if the series should prove infinite—and, ultimately, in its best expression, do so in a cause that means something to thousands, to a people, a nation, to humanity, to God. Nor was there *a test* to show whether or not a pilot had this righteous quality. There was, instead, a seemingly infinite series of tests. A career in flying was like climbing one of those ancient Babylonian pyramids made up of a dizzy progression of steps and ledges, a ziggurat, a pyramid extraordinarily high and steep; and the idea was to prove at every foot of the way up that pyramid that you were one of the elected and anointed ones who had *the right stuff* and could move higher and higher and even—ulti-

mately, God willing, one day—that you might be able to join that special few at the very top, that elite who had the capacity to bring tears to men's eyes, the very Brotherhood of the Right Stuff itself.

None of this was to be mentioned, and yet it was acted out in a way that a young man could not fail to understand. When a new flight (i.e., a class) of trainees arrived at Pensacola, they were brought into an auditorium for a little lecture. An officer would tell them: "Take a look at the man on either side of you." Quite a few actually swiveled their heads this way and that, in the interest of appearing diligent. Then the officer would say: "One of the three of you is not going to make it!"—meaning, not get his wings. That was the opening theme, the *motif* of primary training. We already know that one-third of you do not have the right stuff—it only remains to find out who.

Furthermore, that was the way it turned out. At every level in one's progress up that staggeringly high pyramid, the world was once more divided into those men who had the right stuff to continue the climb and those who had to be *left behind* in the most obvious way. Some were eliminated in the course of the opening classroom work, as either not smart enough or not hardworking enough, and were left behind. Then came the basic flight instruction, in single-engine, propeller-driven trainers, and a few more—even though the military tried to make this stage easy—were washed out and left behind. Then came more demanding levels, one after the other, formation flying, instrument flying, jet training, all-weather flying, gunnery, and at each level more were washed out and left behind. By this point easily a third of the original candidates had been, indeed, eliminated . . . from the ranks of those who might prove to have the right stuff.

In the Navy, in addition to the stages that Air Force trainees went through, the neophyte always had waiting for him, out in the ocean, a certain grim gray slab; namely, the deck of an aircraft carrier; and with it perhaps the most difficult routine in military flying, carrier landings. He was shown films about it, he heard lectures about it, and he knew that carrier landings were hazardous. He first practiced touching down on the shape of a flight deck painted on an airfield. He was instructed to touch down and gun right off. This was safe enough—

the shape didn't move, at least—but it could do terrible things to, let us say, the gyroscope of the soul. *That shape!—it's so damned small!* And more candidates were washed out and left behind. Then came that day, without warning, when those who remained were sent out over the ocean for the first of many days of reckoning with the slab. The first day was always a clear day with little wind and a calm sea. The carrier was so steady that it seemed, from up there in the air, to be resting on pilings, and the candidate usually made his first carrier landing successfully, with relief and even *élan.* Many young candidates looked like terrific aviators up to that very point—and it was not until they were actually standing on the carrier deck that they first began to wonder if they had the proper stuff, after all. In the training film the flight deck was a grand piece of gray geometry, perilous, to be sure, but an amazing abstract shape as one looks down upon it on the screen. And yet once the newcomer's two feet were on it . . . *Geometry*—my God, man, this is a . . . skillet! It *heaved,* it moved up and down underneath his feet, it pitched up, it pitched down, it rolled to port (this great beast *rolled!*) and it rolled to starboard, as the ship moved into the wind and, therefore, into the waves, and the wind kept sweeping across, sixty feet up in the air out in the open sea, and there were no railings whatsoever. This was a *skillet!*—a frying pan!—a short-order grill!—not gray but black, smeared with skid marks from one end to the other and glistening with pools of hydraulic fluid and the occasional jet-fuel slick, all of it still hot, sticky, greasy, runny, virulent from God knows what traumas—still ablaze!—consumed in detonations, explosions, flames, combustion, roars, shrieks, whines, blasts, horrible shudders, fracturing impacts, as little men in screaming red and yellow and purple and green shirts with black Mickey Mouse helmets over their ears skittered about on the surface as if for their very lives (you've said it now!), hooking fighter planes onto the catapult shuttles so that they can explode their afterburners and be slung off the deck in a red-mad fury with a *kaboom!* that pounds through the entire deck—a procedure that seems absolutely controlled, orderly, sublime, however, compared to what he is about to watch as aircraft return to the ship for what is known in the engineering stoicisms of the military as "recovery and arrest." To say that an F-4 was coming back onto this heaving barbecue from out of the sky at a speed of 135 knots . . . that might have been the truth in the training lecture, but it did not begin to get across the idea of what the newcomer saw from the deck itself, because it created the notion that perhaps the plane was gliding in. On the deck one knew differently! As the aircraft came closer and the carrier heaved on into the waves and the plane's speed did not diminish and the deck did not grow steady—indeed, it pitched up and down five or ten feet per greasy heave—one experienced a neural alarm that no lecture could have prepared him for: This is not an *airplane* coming toward me, it is a brick with some poor sonofabitch riding it *(someone much like myself!),* and it is not *gliding,* it is *falling,* a fifty-thousand-pound brick, headed not for a stripe on the deck but for *me*—and with a horrible *smash!* it hits the skillet, and with a blur of momentum as big as a freight train's it hurtles toward the far end of the deck—another blinding storm!—another roar as the pilot pushes the throttle up to full military power and another smear of rubber screams out over the skillet—and this is nominal!—quite okay!—for a wire stretched across the deck has grabbed the hook on the end of the plane as it hit the deck tail down, and the smash was the rest of the fifteen-ton brute slamming onto the deck, as it tripped up, so that it is now straining against the wire at full throttle, in case it hadn't held and the plane had "boltered" off the end of the deck and had to struggle up into the air again. And already the Mickey Mouse helmets are running toward the fiery monster . . .

And the candidate, looking on, begins to *feel* that great heaving sun-blazing deathboard of a deck wallowing in his own vestibular system—and suddenly he finds himself backed up against his own limits. He ends up going to the flight surgeon with so-called conversion symptoms. Overnight he develops blurred vision or numbness in his hands and feet or sinusitis so severe that he cannot tolerate changes in altitude. On one level the symptom is real. He really cannot see too well or use his fingers or stand the pain. But somewhere in his subconscious he knows it is a plea and a beg-off; he shows not the slightest concern (the flight surgeon notes) that the condition might be permanent and affect him in whatever life awaits him outside the arena of the right stuff.

Those who remained, those who qualified for carrier

duty—and even more so those who later on qualified for *night* carrier duty—began to feel a bit like Gideon's warriors. *So many have been left behind!* The young warriors were now treated to a deathly sweet and quite unmentionable sight. They could gaze at length upon the crushed and wilted pariahs who had washed out. They could inspect those who did not have that righeous stuff.

The military did not have very merciful instincts. Rather than packing up these poor souls and sending them home, the Navy, like the Air Force and the Marines, would try to make use of them in some other role, such as flight controller. So the washout has to keep taking classes with the rest of his group, even though he can no longer touch an airplane. He sits there in the classes staring at sheets of paper with cataracts of sheer human mortification over his eyes while the rest steal looks at him . . . this man reduced to an ant, this untouchable, this poor sonofabitch. And in what test had he been found wanting? Why, it seemed to be nothing less than *manhood* itself. Naturally, this was never mentioned, either. Yet there it was. *Manliness, manhood, manly courage* . . . there was something ancient, primordial, irresistible about the challenge of this stuff, no matter what a sophisticated and rational age one might think he lived in.

Perhaps because it could not be talked about, the subject began to take on superstitious and even mystical outlines. A man either had it or he didn't! There was no such thing as having *most* of it. Moreover, it could blow at any seam. One day a man would be ascending the pyramid at a terrific clip, and the next—bingo!—he would reach his own limits in the most unexpected way. Conrad and Schirra met an Air Force pilot who had had a great pal at Tyndall Air Force Base in Florida. This man had been the budding ace of the training class; he had flown the hottest fighter-style trainer, the T-38, like a dream; and then he began the routine step of being checked out in the T-33. The T-33 was not nearly as hot an aircraft as the T-38; it was essentially the old P-80 jet fighter. It had an exceedingly small cockpit. The pilot could barely move his shoulders. It was the sort of airplane of which everybody said, "You don't get into it, you *wear* it." Once inside a T-33 cockpit this man, this budding ace, developed claustrophobia of the most paralyzing sort. He tried everything to overcome it. He

even went to a psychiatrist, which was a serious mistake for a military officer if his superiors learned of it. But nothing worked. He was shifted over to flying jet transports, such as the C-135. Very demanding and necessary aircraft they were, too, and he was still spoken of as an excellent pilot. But as everyone knew—and, again, it was never explained in so many words—only those who were assigned to fighter squadrons, the "fighter jocks," as they called each other with a self-satisfied irony, remained in the true fraternity. Those assigned to transports were not humiliated like washouts—*somebody* had to fly those planes—nevertheless, they, too, had been *left behind* for lack of the right stuff.

Or a man could go for a routine physical one fine day, feeling like a million dollars, and be grounded for *fallen arches*. It happened!—just like that! (And try raising them.) Or for breaking his wrist and losing only *part* of its mobility. Or for a minor deterioration of eyesight, or for any of hundreds of reasons that would make no difference to a man in an ordinary occupation. As a result all fighter jocks began looking upon doctors as their natural enemies. Going to see a flight surgeon was a no-gain proposition; a pilot could only hold his own or lose in the doctor's office. To be grounded for a medical reason was no humiliation, looked at objectively. But it was a humiliation, nonetheless!—for it meant you no longer had that indefinable, unutterable, integral stuff. (It could blow at *any* seam.)

All the hot young fighter jocks began trying to test the limits themselves in a superstitious way. They were like believing Presbyterians of a century before who used to probe their own experience to see if they were truly among *the elect*. When a fighter pilot was in training, whether in the Navy or the Air Force, his superiors were continually spelling out strict rules for him, about the use of the aircraft and conduct in the sky. They repeatedly forbade so-called hot-dog stunts, such as outside loops, buzzing, flat-hatting, hedgehopping and flying under bridges. But somehow one got the message that the man who truly *had* it could ignore those rules—not that he should make a point of it, but that he *could*—and that after all there was only one way to find out—and that in some strange unofficial way, peeking through his fingers, his instructor halfway expected him to challenge all the limits. They would give a lecture about how a pilot should never fly without a good solid breakfast—eggs, bacon, toast, and so forth—because if he tried to fly with his blood-sugar level too low, it could impair his alertness. Naturally, the next day every hot dog in the unit would get up and have a breakfast consisting of one cup of black coffee and take off and go up into a vertical climb until the weight of the ship exactly canceled out the upward pull of the engine and his air speed was zero, and he would hang there for one thick adrenal instant—and then fall like a rock, until one of three things happened: he keeled over nose first and regained his aerodynamics and all was well, he went into a spin and fought his way out of it, or he went into a spin and had to eject or crunch it, which was always supremely possible.

Likewise, "hassling"—mock dogfighting—was strictly forbidden, and so naturally young fighter jocks could hardly wait to go up in, say, a pair of F-100s and start the duel by making a pass at each other at 800 miles an hour, the winner being the pilot who could slip in behind the other one and get locked in on his tail ("wax his tail"), and it was not uncommon for some eager jock to try too tight an outside turn and have his engine flame out, where-upon, unable to restart it, he has to eject . . . and he shakes his fist at the victor as he floats down by parachute and his half-a-million-dollar aircraft goes *kaboom!* on the palmetto grass or the desert floor, and he starts thinking about how he can get together with the other guy back at the base in time for the two of them to get their stories straight before the investigation: "I don't know what happened, sir. I was pulling up after a target run, and it just flamed out on me." Hassling was forbidden, and hassling that led to the destruction of an aircraft was a serious court-martial offense, and the man's superiors knew that the engine hadn't *just flamed out,* but every unofficial impulse on the base seemed to be saying: "Hell, we wouldn't give you a nickel for a pilot who hasn't done some crazy rat-racing like that. It's all part of the right stuff."

The other side of this impulse showed up in the reluctance of the young jocks to admit it when they had maneuvered themselves into a bad corner they couldn't get out of. There were two reasons why a fighter pilot hated to declare an emergency. First, it triggered a complex and very public chain of events at the field: all other incoming flights were held up, including many of one's comrades who were probably low on fuel; the fire trucks came trundling out to the runway like yellow toys (as seen from way up there), the better to illustrate one's hapless state; and the bureaucracy began to crank up the paper monster for the investigation that always followed. And second, to declare an emergency, one first had to reach that conclusion in his own mind, which to the young pilot was the same as saying: "A minute ago I still *had* it—now I need your help!" To have a bunch of young fighter pilots up in the air thinking this way used to drive flight controllers crazy. They would see a ship beginning to drift off the radar, and they couldn't rouse the pilot on the microphone for anything other than a few meaningless mumbles, and they would know he was probably out there with engine failure at a low altitude, trying to reignite by lowering his auxiliary generator rig, which had a little propeller that was supposed to spin in the slipstream like a child's pinwheel.

"Whiskey Kilo Two Eight, do you want to declare an emergency?"

This would rouse him!—to say: "Negative, negative, Whiskey Kilo Two Eight is not declaring an emergency."

Kaboom. Believers in the right stuff would rather crash and burn.

EPILOGUE

Well, the Lord giveth, and the Lord taketh away. After Gordon Cooper's triumph, Alan Shepard had launched a campaign for one more Mercury flight, a three-day mission, which it would be his turn to fly. He had the backing of Walt Williams and most of the astronauts. James Webb headed them off easily, however, with President Kennedy's tacit blessing, and announced that Project Mercury had been completed. NASA and the Administration were having a hard enough time keeping the Congress in line to support the $40 billion Gemini and Apollo lunar-landing programs without prolonging the Mercury series. The spirit of two years before, when Kennedy had raised his arms toward the moon and congressmen cheered and issued forth a limitless budget, had evaporated. The space race was a . . . "race for survival"? The United States faced . . . "national extinction"? Whoever controlled outer space . . . controlled the earth? The Russians were going to . . . put a red spot on the moon? It was impossible to recall the emotion of those days. In mid-June 1963 the Chief Designer (still the anonymous genius!) put *Vostok 5* into orbit with Cosmonaut Valery Bykovsky aboard, and two days later he sent the first woman into space, Cosmonaut Valentina Tereshkova, aboard *Vostok 6,* and they remained in orbit for three days, flying within three miles of each other at one point and landing on Soviet soil on the same day— and not even then did the old sense of warlike urgency revive in the Congress.

In July, Shepard began to be bothered by a ringing in his left ear and occasional dizziness, symptoms of Meunière's syndrome, a disease of the inner ear. Like Slayton, he had to go on inactive status as an astronaut and could only fly an aircraft with a co-pilot aboard. Slayton, meantime, had made a decision that would have been unthinkable to most military officers. He had resigned from the Air Force after nineteen years—one year short of qualifying for the twenty-year-man's pension, that golden reward that blazed out there beyond the horizon throughout the career officer's years of financial hardship. Slayton's problem was that the Air Force had decided to ground him altogether because of his heart condition. As a civilian working for NASA, he could continue to fly high-performance aircraft, so long as he was accompanied by a co-pilot. He could keep up his proficiency, he could remain on flight status, he could keep alive his hopes of proving, somewhere down the line, that he had the right stuff to go aloft as an astronaut, after all. Next to that consideration the pension didn't amount to much.

On July 19 Joe Walker flew the X-15 to 347,800 feet, which was sixty-six miles up, surpassing the record of 314,750 feet set by Bob White the year before; and on August 22 Walker reached 354,200 feet, or sixty-seven miles, which was seventeen miles into space. In addition to White and Walker, one other man had flown the X-15 above fifty miles. That was White's backup, Bob Rushworth, who had achieved 285,000 feet, fifty-four miles, in June. The Air Force had instituted the practice of awarding *Air Force Astronaut* wings to any Air Force pilot who flew above fifty miles. They used the term itself: *astronaut.* As a result, White and Rushworth, the Air Force's prime and backup pilots for the X-15, now had

their astronaut wings. Joe Walker, being a civilian flying the X-15 for NASA, did not qualify. So some of Walker's good buddies at Edwards took him out to a restaurant for dinner, and they all knocked back a few, and they pinned some cardboard wings on his chest. The inscription read: "Asstronaut."

On September 28 the seven Mercury astronauts went to Los Angeles for the awards banquet of the Society of Experimental Test Pilots. Iven Kincheloe's widow, Dorothy, presented them with the Iven C. Kincheloe Award for outstanding professional performance in the conduct of flight test. The wire services devoted scarcely more than a paragraph to the occasion, and that they took from the handout. After all the Distinguished Service Medals and the parades and the appearances before Congress, after every sort of tribute that politicians, private institutions, and the Genteel Beast could devise, the Iven C. Kincheloe Award didn't seem like very much. But for the seven astronauts it was an important night. The radiant Kinch, the great blond movie-star picture of a pilot, was the most famous of the dead rocket pilots and could have cut his own orders in the Air Force, had he lived. He would have had Bob White's job as prime pilot of the X-15 and God knows what else. There were aviation awards and aviation awards, but the Kincheloe Award— for "professional performance"—was the big one within the flight test fraternity. The seven men had finally closed the circle and brought together the scattered glories of their celebrity. They had fought for a true pilot's role in Project Mercury, they had won it, step by step, and Cooper's flight, on top of the others, had shown they could handle it in the classic way, out on the edge. Now they had the one thing that had been denied them for years while the rest of the nation worshipped them so unquestioningly: acceptance by their peers, their true brethren, as *test pilots* of the space age, deserving occupants of the top of the pyramid of the right stuff.

During the summer Kennedy had gone on television to tell the nation that a nuclear test ban agreement with the Russians had been reached. Thereupon the Soviet foreign minister, Andrei Gromyko, had proposed a corollary that would ban even the placing of nuclear weapons in earth orbit. The Soviets themselves were extinguishing the notion of the thunderbolts from space. On August 30 there had gone into service the piece of equipment by which the entire interlude would be remembered: the hotline, a telephone hookup between the White House and the Kremlin, the better to avoid misunderstandings that might result in nuclear war. When Kennedy was assassinated on November 22 by a man with Russian and Cuban ties, there was no anti-Soviet or anti-Cuban clamor in the Congress or in the press. The Cold War, as anyone could plainly see, was over.

No one, and certainly not the men themselves, could comprehend the meaning of this for the role of *the astronaut,* however. The new President, Lyndon Johnson, proved to be even more of a proponent of the space program than his predecessor. Due partly to the political genius of James E. Webb, who now came into his own, the Congress swung about and gave NASA a blank check for the missions to the moon. Nevertheless, the fact remained: the Cold War was over.

No more manned spaceflights were scheduled until the start of the Gemini program in 1965. By then the seven Mercury astronauts would begin to feel a change in the public attitude toward them and, for that matter, toward the Next Nine and the groups of astronauts that were to follow. They would *feel* the change, but they would not be able to put it into words. What *was* that feeling? Why, it was the gentle slither of the mantle of soldierly glory sliding off one's shoulders!—and the cooling effect of oceans of tears drying up! The single-combat warriors' war had been removed. They would continue to be honored, and men would continue to be awed by their courage; but the day when an astronaut could parade up Broadway while traffic policemen wept in the intersections was no more. Never again would an astronaut be perceived as a protector of the people, risking his life to do battle in the heavens. Not even the first American to walk on the moon would ever know the outpouring of a people's most primal emotions that Shepard, Cooper, and, above all, Glenn had known. The era of America's first single-combat warriors had come, and it had gone, perhaps never to be relived.

The Lord giveth, and the Lord taketh away. The mantle of Cold Warrior of the Heavens had been placed on their shoulders one April day in 1959 without their asking for it or having anything to do with it or even knowing it. And now it would be taken away, without their knowing that, either, and because of nothing they ever did or desired. John Glenn had made up his mind to run for the Senate in Ohio in 1964. He could not have foreseen that the voters of Ohio would no longer regard him as a man with a protector's aura. But at least he would be remembered. It would have been still more impossible for his confreres to realize that the day might come when Americans would hear their names and say, "Oh, yes—now, which one was he?"

From PROFILES IN COURAGE

John F. Kennedy

". . . not as a Massachusetts man
but as an American . . ."
—Daniel Webster

The blizzardy night of January 21, 1850, was no night in Washington for an ailing old man to be out. But wheezing and coughing fitfully, Henry Clay made his way through the snowdrifts to the home of Daniel Webster. He had a plan—a plan to save the Union—and he knew he must have the support of the North's most renowned orator and statesman. He knew that he had no time to lose, for that very afternoon President Taylor, in a message to Congress asking California's admission as a free state, had only thrown fuel on the raging fire that threatened to consume the Union. Why had the President failed to mention New Mexico, asked the North? What about the Fugitive Slave Law being enforced, said the South? What about the District of Columbia slave trade, Utah, Texas boundaries? Tempers mounted, plots unfolded, disunity was abroad in the land.

But Henry Clay had a plan—a plan for another Great Compromise to preserve the nation. For an hour he outlined its contents to Daniel Webster in the warmth of the latter's comfortable home, and together they talked of saving the Union. Few meetings in American history have ever been so productive or so ironic in their consequences. For the Compromise of 1850 added to Henry Clay's garlands as the great Pacificator; but Daniel Webster's support which insured its success resulted in his political crucifixion, and, for half a century or more, his historical condemnation.

The man upon whom Henry Clay called that wintry night was one of the most extraordinary figures in American political history. Daniel Webster is familiar to many of us today as the battler for Jabez Stone's soul against the devil in Stephen Vincent Benét's story. But in his own lifetime, he had many battles against the devil for his own soul—and some he lost. Webster, wrote one of his intimate friends, was "a compound of strength and weakness, dust and divinity," or in Emerson's words, "a great man with a small ambition."

There could be no mistaking he was a great man—he looked like one, talked like one, was treated like one and insisted he was one. With all his faults and failings, Daniel Webster was undoubtedly the most talented figure in our Congressional history: not in his ability to win men to a cause—he was no match in that with Henry Clay; not in his ability to hammer out a philosophy of government—Calhoun outshone him there; but in his ability to make alive and supreme the latent sense of oneness, of Union, that all Americans felt but which few could express.

But how Daniel Webster could express it! How he could express almost any sentiments! Ever since his first speech in Congress—attacking the War of 1812—had riveted the attention of the House of Representatives as no freshman had ever held it before, he was the outstanding orator of his day—indeed, of all time—in Congress, before hushed throngs in Massachusetts and as an advocate before the Supreme Court. Stern Chief Justice Marshall was said to have been visibly moved by Webster's famous defense in the Dartmouth college case—"It is, sir, as I have said, a small college—and yet there are those who love it." After his oration on the two hundredth founding of Plymouth Colony, a young Harvard scholar wrote:

> I was never so excited by public speaking before in my life. Three or four times I thought my temple would burst with the rush of blood. . . . I was beside myself and I am still so.

And the peroration of his reply to Senator Hayne of South Carolina, when secession had threatened twenty years earlier, was a national rallying cry memorized by every schoolboy—"Liberty and Union, now and forever, one and inseparable!"

A very slow speaker, hardly averaging a hundred words a minute, Webster combined the musical charm of his deep organ-like voice, a vivid imagination, an ability to crush his opponents with a barrage of facts, a confident and deliberate manner of speaking and a striking appearance to make his orations a magnet that drew crowds hurrying to the Senate chamber. He prepared his speeches with the utmost care, but seldom wrote them out in a prepared text. It has been said that he could think out a speech sentence by sentence, correct the sentences in his mind without the use of a pencil and then deliver it exactly as he thought it out.

Certainly that striking appearance was half the secret of his power, and convinced all who looked upon his face that he was one born to rule men. Although less than six feet tall, Webster's slender frame when contrasted with the magnificent sweep of his shoulders gave him a theatrical but formidable presence. But it was his extraordinary head that contemporaries found so memorable, with the features Carlyle described for all to remember: "The tanned complexion, the amorphous crag-like face; the dull black eyes under the precipice of brows, like dull anthracite furnaces needing only to be blown; the mastiff mouth accurately closed." One contemporary called Webster "a living lie, because no man on earth could be so great as he looked."

And Daniel Webster was not as great as he looked. The flaw in the granite was the failure of his moral senses to develop as acutely as his other faculties. He could see nothing improper in writing to the President of the Bank of the United States—at the very time when the Senate was engaged in debate over a renewal of the Bank's charter—noting that "my retainer has not been received or refreshed as usual." But Webster accepted favors not as gifts but as services which he believed were rightly due him. When he tried to resign from the Senate in 1836 to recoup speculative losses through his law practice, his Massachusetts businessmen friends joined to pay his debts to retain him in office. Even at his deathbed, legend tells us, there was a knock at his door, and a large roll of bills was thrust in by an old gentleman, who said that "At such a time as this, there should be no shortage of money in the house."

Webster took it all and more. What is difficult to comprehend is that he saw no wrong in it—morally or otherwise. He probably believed that he was greatly underpaid, and it never occurred to him that by his own free choice he had sold his services and his talents, however extraordinary they might have been, to the people of the United States, and no one else, when he drew his salary as United States Senator. But Webster's support of the business interests of New England was not the result of the money he obtained, but of his personal convictions. Money meant little to him except as a means to gratify his peculiar tastes. He never accumulated a fortune. He never was out of debt. And he never was troubled by his debtor status. Sometimes he paid, and he always did so when it was convenient, but as Gerald W. Johnson says, "Unfortunately he sometimes paid in the wrong coin—not in legal tender—but in the confidence that the people reposed in him."

But whatever his faults, Daniel Webster remained the greatest orator of his day, the leading member of the American Bar, one of the most renowned leaders of the Whig party, and the only Senator capable of checking Calhoun. And thus Henry Clay knew he must enlist these extraordinary talents on behalf of his Great Compromise. Time and events proved he was right.

As the God-like Daniel listened in thoughtful silence, the sickly Clay unfolded his last great effort to hold the Union together. Its key features were five in number: (1) California was to be admitted as a free (nonslaveholding) state; (2) New Mexico and Utah were to be organized as territories without legislation either for or against slavery, thus running directly contrary to the hotly debated Wilmot Proviso which was intended to prohibit slavery in the new territories; (3) Texas was to be compensated for some territory to be ceded to New Mexico; (4) the slave trade would be abolished in the District of Columbia; and (5) a more stringent and enforceable Fugitive Slave Law was to be enacted to guarantee return to their masters of runaway slaves captured in Northern states. The Compromise would be condemned by the Southern extremists as appeasement, chiefly on its first and fourth provisions; and by the Northern abolitionists as 90 per cent concessions to the South with a meaningless 10 per cent sop thrown to the North, particularly because of the second and fifth provisions. Few Northerners could stomach any strengthening of the Fugitive Slave Act, the most bitterly hated measure—and until prohibition, the most flagrantly disobeyed—ever passed by Congress. Massachusetts had even enacted a law making it a crime for anyone to enforce the provisions of the Act in that state!

How could Henry Clay then hope to win to such a plan Daniel Webster of Massachusetts? Was he not specifically on record as a consistent foe of slavery and a supporter of the Wilmot Proviso? Had he not told the Senate in the Oregon Debate:

> I shall oppose all slavery extension and all increase of slave respresentation in all places, at all times, under all circumstances, even against all inducements, against all supposed limitation of great interests, against all combinations, against all compromises.

That very week he had written a friend: "From my earliest youth, I have regarded slavery as a great moral and political evil. . . . You need not fear that I shall vote for any compromise or do anything inconsistent with the past."

But Daniel Webster feared that civil violence "would only rivet the chains of slavery the more strongly." And the preservation of the Union was far dearer to his heart than his opposition to slavery.

And thus on that fateful January night, Daniel Webster promised Henry Clay his conditional support, and took inventory of the crisis about him. At first he shared the views of those critics and historians who scoffed at the possibility of secession in 1850. But as he talked with Southern leaders and observed "the condition of the country, I thought the inevitable consequences of leaving the existing controversies unadjusted would be Civil War." "I am nearly broken down with labor and anxiety," he wrote his son, "I know not how to meet the present emergency, or with what weapons to beat down the Northern and Southern follies now raging in equal extremes. . . . I have poor spirits and little courage."

Two groups were threatening in 1850 to break away from the United States of America. In New England, Garrison was publicly proclaiming, "I am an Abolitionist and, therefore, for the dissolution of the Union." And a mass meeting of Northern Abolitionists declared that "the Constitution is a covenant with death and an agreement with hell." In the South, Calhoun was writing a friend in February of 1850, "Disunion is the only alternative that is left for us." And in his last great address to the Senate, read for him on March 4, only a few short weeks before his death, while he sat by too feeble to speak, he declared, "The South will be forced to choose between abolition and secession."

A preliminary convention of Southerners, also instigated by Calhoun, urged a full-scale convention of the South at Nashville for June of that fateful year to popularize the idea of dissolution.

The time was ripe for secession, and few were prepared to speak for Union. Even Alexander Stephens of Georgia, anxious to preserve the Union, wrote friends in the South who were sympathetic with his views that "the feeling among the Southern members for a dissolution of the Union . . . is becoming much more general. Men are now beginning to talk of it seriously who twelve months ago hardly permitted themselves to think of it . . . the crisis is not far ahead. . . . A dismemberment of this Republic I now consider inevitable." During the critical month preceding Webster's speech, six Southern states, each to secede ten years later, approved the aims of the Nashville Convention and appointed delegates. Horace Greeley wrote on February 23:

> There are sixty members of Congress who this day desire and are plotting to effect the idea of a dissolution of the Union. We have no doubt the Nashville Convention will be held and that the leading purpose of its authors is the separation of the slave states . . . with the formation of an independent confederacy.

Such was the perilous state of the nation in the early months of 1850.

By the end of February, the Senator from Massachusetts had determined upon his course. Only the Clay Compromise, Daniel Webster decided, could avert secession and civil war; and he wrote a friend that he planned "to make an honest truth-telling speech and a Union speech, and discharge a clear conscience." As he set to work preparing his notes, he received abundant warning of the attacks his message would provoke. His constituents and Massachusetts newspapers admonished him strongly not to waver in his consistent anti-slavery stand, and many urged him to employ still tougher tones against the South. But the Senator from Massachusetts had made up his mind, as he told his friends on March 6, "to push my skiff from the shore alone." He would act according to the creed with which he had challenged the Senate several years earlier:

Inconsistencies of opinion arising from changes of circumstances are often justifiable. But there is one sort of inconsistency that is culpable: it is the inconsistency between a man's conviction and his vote, between his conscience and his conduct. No man shall ever charge me with an inconsistency of that kind.

And so came the 7th of March, 1850, the only day in history which would become the title of a speech delivered on the Senate floor. No one recalls today—no one even recalled in 1851—the formal title Webster gave his address, for it had become the "Seventh of March" speech as much as Independence Day is known as the Fourth of July.

Realizing after months of insomnia that this might be the last great effort his health would permit, Webster stimulated his strength for the speech by oxide of arsenic and other drugs, and devoted the morning to polishing up his notes. He was excitedly interrupted by the Sergeant at Arms, who told him that even then—two hours before the Senate was to meet—the chamber, the galleries, the anterooms and even the corridors of the Capitol were filled with those who had been traveling for days from all parts of the nation to hear Daniel Webster. Many foreign diplomats and most of the House of Representatives were among those vying for standing room. As the Senate met, members could scarcely walk to their seats through the crowd of spectators and temporary seats made of public documents stacked on top of each other. Most Senators gave up their seats to ladies, and stood in the aisles awaiting Webster's opening blast.

As the Vice President's gavel commenced the session, Senator Walker of Wisconsin, who held the floor to finish a speech begun the day before, told the Chair that "this vast audience has not come to hear me, and there is but one man who can assemble such an audience. They expect to hear him, and I feel it is my duty, as it is my pleasure, to give the floor to the Senator from Massachusetts."

The crowd fell silent as Daniel Webster rose slowly to his feet, all the impressive powers of his extraordinary physical appearance—the great, dark, brooding eyes, the wonderfully bronzed complexion, the majestic domed forehead—commanding the same awe they had commanded for more than thirty years. Garbed in his familiar blue tailed coat with brass buttons, and a buff waistcoat and breeches, he deliberately paused a moment as he gazed about at the greatest assemblage of Senators ever to gather in that chamber—Clay, Benton, Houston, Jefferson Davis, Hale, Bell, Cass, Seward, Chase, Stephen A. Douglas and others. But one face was missing—that of the ailing John C. Calhoun.

All eyes were fixed on the speaker; no spectator save his own son knew what he would say. "I have never before," wrote a newspaper correspondent, "witnessed an occasion on which there was deeper feeling enlisted or more universal anxiety to catch the most distinct echo of the speaker's voice."

In his moments of magnificent inspiration, as Emerson once described him, Webster was truly "the great cannon loaded to the lips." Summoning for the last time that spellbinding oratorical ability, he abandoned his previous opposition to slavery in the territories, abandoned his constituents' abhorrence of the Fugitive Slave Law, abandoned his own place in the history and hearts of his countrymen and abandoned his last chance for the goal that had eluded him for over twenty years—the Presidency. Daniel Webster preferred to risk his career and his reputation rather than risk the Union.

"Mr. President," he began, "I wish to speak today, not as a Massachusetts man, nor as a Northern man, but as an American and a Member of the Senate of the United States. . . . I speak today for the preservation of the Union. Hear me for my cause."

He had spoken but for a short time when the gaunt, bent form of Calhoun, wrapped in a black cloak, was dramatically assisted into his seat, where he sat trembling, scarcely able to move, and unnoticed by the speaker. After several expressions of regret by Webster that illness prevented the distinguished Senator from South Carolina from being present, Calhoun struggled up, grasping the arms of his chair, and in a clear and ghostly voice proudly announced, "The Senator from South Carolina *is* in his seat." Webster was touched, and with tears in his eyes he extended a bow toward Calhoun, who sank back exhausted and feeble, eyeing the Massachusetts orator with a sphinx-like expression which disclosed no hint of either approval or disapproval.

For three hours and eleven minutes, with only a few references to his extensive notes, Daniel Webster pleaded the Union's cause. Relating the grievances of each side, he asked for conciliation and understanding in the name of patriotism. The Senate's main concern, he insisted, was neither to promote slavery nor to abolish it, but to preserve the United States of America. And with telling logic and remarkable foresight he bitterly attacked the idea of "peaceable secession":

> Sir, your eyes and mine are never destined to see that miracle. The dismemberment of this vast country without convulsion. Who is so foolish . . . as to expect to see any such thing? . . . Instead of speaking of the possibility or utility of secession, instead of dwelling in those caverns of darkness, . . . let us enjoy the fresh air of liberty and union. . . . Let us make our generation one of the strongest and brightest links in that golden chain which is destined, I fondly believe, to grapple the people of all the states to this Constitution for ages to come.

There was no applause. Buzzing and astonished whispering, yes, but no applause. Perhaps his hearers were too intent—or too astonished. A reporter rushed to the telegraph office. "Mr. Webster has assumed a great responsibility," he wired his paper, "and whether he succeeds or fails, the courage with which he has come forth at least entitles him to the respect of the country."

Daniel Webster did succeed. Even though his speech was repudiated by many in the North, the very fact that one who represented such a belligerent constituency would appeal for understanding in the name of unity and patriotism was recognized in Washington and throughout the South as a *bona fide* assurance of Southern rights. Despite Calhoun's own intransigence, his Charleston *Mercury* praised Webster's address as "noble in language, generous and conciliatory in tone. Mr. Calhoun's clear and powerful exposition would have had something of a decisive effect if it had not been so soon followed by Mr. Webster's masterly playing." And the New Orleans *Picayune* hailed Webster for "the moral courage to do what he believes to be just in itself and necessary for the peace and safety of the country."

And so the danger of immediate secession and bloodshed passed. As Senator Winthrop remarked, Webster's speech had "disarmed and quieted the South [and] knocked the Nashville Convention into a cocked hat." The *Journal of Commerce* was to remark in later months that "Webster did more than any other man in the whole country, and at a greater hazard of personal popularity, to stem and roll back the torrent of sectionalism which in 1850 threatened to overthrow the pillars of the Constitution and the Union."

Some historians—particularly those who wrote in the latter half of the nineteenth century under the influence of the moral earnestness of Webster's articulate Abolitionist foes—do not agree with Allan Nevins, Henry Steele Commager, Gerald Johnson and others who have praised the Seventh of March speech as "the highest statesmanship . . . Webster's last great service to the nation." Many deny that secession would have occurred in 1850 without such compromises; and others maintain that subsequent events proved eventual secession was inevitable regardless of what compromises were made. But still others insist that delaying war for ten years narrowed the issues between North and South and in the long run helped preserve the Union. The spirit of conciliation in Webster's speech gave the North the righteous feeling that it had made every attempt to treat the South with fairness, and the defenders of the Union were thus united more strongly against what they felt to be Southern violations of those compromises ten years later. Even from the military point of view of the North, postponement of the battle for ten years enabled the Northern states to increase tremendously their lead in popularity, voting power, production and railroads.

Undoubtedly this was understood by many of Webster's supporters, including the business and professional men of Massachusetts who helped distribute hundreds of thousands of copies of the Seventh of March speech throughout the country. It was understood by Daniel Webster, who dedicated the printed copies to the people of Massacusetts with these words: "Necessity compels me to speak true rather than pleasing things. . . . I should indeed like to please you, but I prefer to save you, whatever be your attitude toward me."

But it was not understood by the Abolitionists and

Free Soilers of 1850. Few politicians have had the distinction of being scourged by such talented constituents. The Rev. Theodore Parker, heedless of the dangers of secession, who had boasted of harboring a fugitive slave in his cellar and writing his sermons with a sword over his ink stand and a pistol in his desk "loaded and ready for defense," denounced Webster in merciless fashion from his pulpit, an attack he would continue even after Webster's death: "No living man has done so much," he cried, "to debauch the conscience of the nation. . . . I know of no deed in American history done by a son of New England to which I can compare this, but the act of Benedict Arnold." "Webster," said Horace Mann, "is a fallen star! Lucifer descending from Heaven!" Longfellow asked the world: "Is it possible? Is this the Titan who hurled mountains at Hayne years ago?" And Emerson proclaimed that "Every drop of blood in that man's veins has eyes that look downward. . . . Webster's absence of moral faculty is degrading to the country." To William Cullen Bryant, Webster was "a man who has deserted the cause which he lately defended, and deserted it under circumstances which force upon him the imputation of a sordid motive." And to James Russell Lowell he was "the most meanly and foolishly treacherous man I ever heard of."

Charles Sumner, who would be elevated to the Senate upon his departure, enrolled the name of Webster on "the dark list of apostates. Mr. Webster's elaborate treason has done more than anything else to break down the North." Senator William H. Seward, the brilliant "Conscience" Whig, called Webster a "traitor to the cause of freedom." A mass meeting in Faneuil Hall condemned the speech as "unworthy of a wise statesman and a good man," and resolved that "Constitution or no Constitution, law or no law, we will not allow a fugitive slave to be taken from the state of Massachusetts." As the Massachusetts Legislature enacted further resolutions wholly contrary to the spirit of the Seventh of March speech, one member called Webster "a recreant son of Massachusetts who misrepresents her in the Senate"; and another stated that "Daniel Webster will be a fortunate man if God, in his sparing mercy, shall preserve his life long enough for him to repent of this act and efface this strain on his name."

The Boston *Courier* pronounced that it was "unable to find that any Northern Whig member of Congress concurs with Mr. Webster"; and his old defender, the Boston *Atlas* stated, "His sentiments are not our sentiments nor we venture to say of the Whigs of New England." The New York *Tribune* considered it "unequal to the occasion and unworthy of its author"; the New York *Evening Post* spoke in terms of a "traitorous retreat . . . a man who deserted the cause which he lately defended"; and the Abolitionist press called it "the scarlet infamy of Daniel Webster. . . . An indescribably base and wicked speech."

Edmund Quincy spoke bitterly of the "ineffable meanness of the lion turned spaniel in his fawnings on the masters whose hands he was licking for the sake of the dirty puddings they might have to toss to him." And finally, the name of Daniel Webster was humiliated for all time in the literature of our land by the cutting words of the usually gentle John Greenleaf Whittier in his immortal poem "Ichabod":

> So fallen! so lost! the light withdrawn
> Which once he wore!
> The glory from his gray hairs gone
> Forevermore! . . .
>
> Of all we loved and honored, naught
> Save power remains;
> A fallen angel's pride of thought,
> Still strong in chains. . . .
>
> Then pay the reverence of old days
> To his dead fame;
> Walk backward, with averted gaze,
> And hide the shame!

Years afterward Whittier was to recall that he penned this acid verse "in one of the saddest moments of my life." And for Daniel Webster, the arrogant, scornful giant of the ages who believed himself above political rancor, Whittier's attack was especially bitter. To some extent he had attempted to shrug off his attackers, stating that he had expected to be libeled and abused, particularly by the Abolitionists and intellectuals who had previously scorned him, much as George Washington and others before him had been abused. To those who urged a prompt reply, he merely related the story of the old deacon in a similar predicament who told his friends, "I always make it a rule never to clean up the path until the snow is done falling."

But he was saddened by the failure of a single other New England Whig to rise to his defense, and he remarked that he was

> engaged in a controversy in which I have neither a leader nor a follower from among my own immediate friends. . . . I am tired of standing up here, almost alone from Massachusetts, contending for practical measures absolutely essential to the good of the country. . . . For five months . . . no one of my colleagues manifested the slightest concurrence in my sentiments. . . . Since the 7th of March there has not been an hour in which I have not felt a crushing weight of anxiety. I have sat down to no breakfast or dinner to which I have brought an unconcerned and easy mind.

But, although he sought to explain his objectives and reassure his friends of his continued opposition to slavery, he nevertheless insisted he would

> stand on the principle of my speech to the end. . . . If necessary I will take the stump in every village in New England. . . . What is to come of the present commotion in men's minds I cannot foresee; but my own convictions of duty are fixed and strong, and I shall continue to follow those convictions without faltering. . . . In highly excited times it is far easier to fan and feed the flames of discord, than to subdue them; and he who counsels moderation is in danger of being regarded as failing in his duty to his party.

And the following year, despite his seventy years, Webster went on extended speaking tours defending his position. "If the chances had been one in a thousand that Civil War would be the result, I should still have felt that thousandth chance should be guarded against by any reasonable sacrifice." When his efforts—and those of Clay, Douglas and others—on behalf of compromise were ultimately successful, he noted sarcastically that many of his colleagues were now saying "They always meant to stand by the Union to the last."

But Daniel Webster was doomed to disappointment in his hopes that this latent support might again enable him to seek the Presidency. For his speech had so thoroughly destroyed those prospects that the recurring popularity of his position could not possibly satisfy the great masses of voters in New England and the North. He could not receive the Presidential nomination he had so long desired; but neither could he ever put to rest the assertion, which was not only expressed by his contemporary critics but subsequently by several nineteenth-century historians, that his real objective in the Seventh of March speech was a bid for Southern support for the Presidency.

But this "profound selfishness," which Emerson was so certain the speech represented, could not have entered into Daniel Webster's motivations. "Had he been bidding for the Presidency," as Professor Nevins points out, "he would have trimmed his phrases and inserted weasel-words upon New Mexico and the fugitive slaves. The first precaution of any aspirant for the Presidency is to make sure of his own state and section; and Webster knew that his speech would send echoes of denunciation leaping from Mount Mansfield to Monamoy Light." Moreover, Webster was sufficiently acute politically to know that a divided party such as his would turn away from politically controversial figures and move to an uncommitted neutral individual, a principle consistently applied to this day. And the 1852 Whig Convention followed exactly this course. After the procompromise vote had been divided for fifty-two ballots between Webster and President Fillmore, the convention turned to the popular General Winfield Scott. Not a single Southern Whig supported Webster. And when the Boston Whigs urged that the party platform take credit for the Clay Compromise, of which, they said, "Daniel Webster, with the concurrence of Henry Clay and other profound statesmen, was the author," Senator Corwin of Ohio was reported to have commented sarcastically, "And I, with the concurrence of Moses, and some extra help, wrote the Ten Commandments."

So Daniel Webster, who neither could have intended his speech as an improvement of his political popularity nor permitted his ambitions to weaken his plea for the

Union, died a disappointed and discouraged death in 1852, his eyes fixed on the flag flying from the mast of the sailboat he had anchored in view of his bedroom window. But to the very end he was true to character, asking on his deathbed, "Wife, children, doctor, I trust on this occasion I have said nothing unworthy of Daniel Webster." And to the end he had been true to the Union, and to his greatest act of courageous principle; for in his last words to the Senate, Webster had written his own epitaph:

I shall stand by the Union . . . with absolute disregard of personal consequences. What are personal consequences . . . in comparison with the good or evil which may befall a great country in a crisis like this? . . . Let the consequences be what they will, I am careless. No man can suffer too much, and no man can fall too soon, if he suffer or if he fall in defense of the liberties and Constitution of his country.

All the illustrations by Norman Rockwell in this book, with the exception of seven, are reprinted by arrangement with the Estate of Norman Rockwell. Copyright © 1917, 1918, 1919, 1920, 1922, 1923, 1924, 1926, 1927, 1928, 1929, 1930, 1931, 1934, 1935, 1936, 1939, 1941, 1942, 1943, 1944, 1945, 1946, 1948, 1956, 1958, 1959, 1960, 1961, 1962, 1963 by The Curtis Publishing Company. Copyright renewed 1945, 1946, 1947, 1948, 1950, 1951, 1952, 1954, 1955, 1956, 1957, 1958, 1959, 1962, 1963, 1964, 1967, 1969, 1970, 1971, 1972, 1973, 1974, 1975, 1976, 1984 by The Curtis Publishing Company. Illustration on page 35, copyright © 1928, 1956 Estate of Norman Rockwell. By permission of the Estate of Norman Rockwell.

The *Four Seasons* illustration art, which appears on pages 51, 89, 92, 127, 142, 183, and the frontispiece are from the archives of Brown and Bigelow. Reprinted by permission of Brown and Bigelow.

Grateful acknowledgment is made to the following for permission to reprint copyrighted material:

Harry N. Abrams, Inc.: A selection from *Norman Rockwell's Americana: ABC* by George Mendoza, published 1975 by Harry N. Abrams, Inc. © 1975 by Harry N. Abrams, Inc., New York.

Brandt & Brandt Literary Agents Inc.: An excerpt from "Abraham Lincoln" by Rosemary and Stephen Vincent Benét from *A Book of Americans* by Rosemary and Stephen Vincent Benét, copyright 1933 by Rosemary and Stephen Vincent Benét. Copyright renewed © 1961 by Rosemary Carr Benét. "John Brown's Body" by Stephen Vincent Benét from *The Selected Works of Stephen Vincent Benét*, Holt, Rinehart and Winston, Inc., copyright 1927, 1928 by Stephen Vincent Benét. Copyright renewed 1955, 1956 by Rosemary Carr Benét. Reprinted by permission of Brandt & Brandt Literary Agents Inc.

Coward, McCann & Geoghegan, Inc.: *Mr. Lincoln's Whiskers* by Burke Davis. Text copyright © 1978 by Burke Davis. Reprinted by permission of Coward, McCann & Geoghegan, Inc.

Walt Disney Music Company: Excerpt from "Zip-A-Dee-Doo-Dah." © 1945 Walt Disney Music Company. Words by Ray Gilbert, music by Allie Wrubel.

E. P. Dutton: "Races" by Rosalind Franklin from *The World from My Window*, edited by George Mendoza. Copyright © 1969 by George Mendoza. A Hawthorn Book. "America the Beautiful" from *Poems* by Katherine Lee Bates. Reprinted by permission of the publisher, E. P. Dutton, a division of New American Library.

Farrar, Straus & Giroux, Inc., and International Creative Management, Inc.: Excerpts from *The Right Stuff* by Tom Wolfe. Copyright © 1979 by Tom Wolfe. Reprinted by permission of Farrar, Straus & Giroux, Inc., and International Creative Management, Inc.

Garrard Publishing Company: A selection from *The Story of the United States Flag* by Wyatt Blassingame. Copyright 1969 by Wyatt Blassingame. Reprinted with the permission of Garrard Publishing Company, Champaign, Illinois.

Harcourt Brace Jovanovich, Inc.: "The People Will Live On" from *The People, Yes* by Carl Sandburg. Copyright 1936 by Harcourt Brace Jovanovich, Inc.; renewed 1964 by Carl Sandburg. "Threes" from *Smoke and Steel* by Carl Sandburg. Copyright 1920 by Harcourt Brace Jovanovich, Inc.; renewed 1948 by Carl Sandburg. "Cool Tombs" from *Cornhuskers* by Carl Sandburg. Copyright 1918 by Holt, Rinehart and Winston, Inc.; renewed 1946 by Carl Sandburg. "Reveille" from *These Times* by Louis Untermeyer. Copyright 1917, 1945 by Louis Untermeyer. Reprinted by permission of Harcourt Brace Jovanovich, Inc.

Harper & Row, Publishers, Inc.: Chapter 3, "Daniel Webster," from *Profiles in Courage* by John F.

Kennedy. Copyright © 1955, 1956 by John F. Kennedy. Reprinted by permission of Harper & Row, Publishers, Inc.

Holt, Rinehart and Winston, Publishers: "Victory Bells" from *Wilderness Songs* by Grace Hazard Conkling. Copyright 1920 by Holt, Rinehart and Winston. Copyright 1948 by Grace Hazard Conkling. Reprinted by permission of Holt, Rinehart and Winston, Publishers.

Holt, Rinehart and Winston, Publishers, and Jonathan Cape Ltd.: "The Gift Outright" from *The Poetry of Robert Frost*, edited by Edward Connery Lathem. Copyright 1942 by Robert Frost. Copyright © 1969 by Holt, Rinehart and Winston. Copyright © 1970 by Lesley Frost Ballantine. Reprinted by permission of Holt, Rinehart and Winston, Publishers, and Jonathan Cape Ltd.

Houghton Mifflin Company: "Brave New World" from *New and Collected Poems 1917–1976* by Archibald MacLeish. Copyright © 1976 by Archibald MacLeish. Reprinted by permission of Houghton Mifflin Company. "Our Country" from *Sunset Ridge: Poems Old and New* by Julia Ward Howe. "The Building of a Ship" from *The Poetical Works of Henry Wadsworth Longfellow*. "Freedom" from *The Poetical Works of James Russell Lowell*. "Concord Hymn" by Ralph Waldo Emerson *(Poems, 1867)*. "Our Intellectual Declaration of Independence" by Ralph Waldo Emerson. Originally published by Houghton Mifflin Company.

Alfred A. Knopf, Inc.: "Dreams" from *The Dream Keeper and Other Poems* by Langston Hughes. Copyright 1932 by Alfred A. Knopf, Inc., and renewed 1960 by Langston Hughes. Reprinted by permission of Alfred A. Knopf, Inc.

Little, Brown and Company: A selection from *Blue Highways: A Journey into America* by William Least Heat Moon. Copyright © 1982 by William Least Heat Moon. By permission of Little, Brown and Company in association with the Atlantic Monthly Press. A selection from *The American Dream* by James Truslow Adams used by permission of the publisher, Little, Brown and Company.

Liveright Publishing Corporation: "Proem: To Brooklyn Bridge" is reprinted from *The Complete Poems and Selected Letters and Prose of Hart Crane*, edited by Brom Weber, by permission of Liveright Publishing Corporation. Copyright 1933, © 1958, 1966 by Liveright Publishing Corporation.

The MIT Press: From "The American Character" by George Santayana, *The Definitive Edition of the Works of George Santayana*, edited by H. J. Saatkamp, Jr., and William G. Holzberg. Published by The MIT Press.

The New York Times Company: "Flag Day—1940," an editorial of June 14, 1940. Copyright © 1940 by The New York Times Company. Reprinted by permission.

The Putnam Publishing Group: "God Doesn't Vote," "Why Are People Mumbling?," "The Thrill Is Gone," and "The Fashion Capital" reprinted by permission of The Putnam Publishing Group from *Laid Back in Washington* by Art Buchwald. Copyright © 1978, 1979, 1980, 1981 by Art Buchwald.

Random House, Inc., and Faber and Faber Ltd.: "The Unknown Citizen," copyright 1940 and renewed 1968 by W. H. Auden. Reprinted from *W. H. Auden: Collected Poems* by W. H. Auden, edited by Edward Mendelson, by permission of Random House, Inc., and Faber and Faber Ltd.

The Estate of Norman Rockwell: Selection from *Norman Rockwell: My Adventures as an Illustrator.* Copyright © 1960 by the Estate of Norman Rockwell. By permission of the Estate of Norman Rockwell.

Theodore Roosevelt Association: "High of Heart" by Theodore Roosevelt and Theodore Roosevelt's letter written on *The Outlook* stationery.

Ann Kaufman Schneider: "German-Americans" from *The American Way* by George S. Kaufman and Moss Hart. Copyright 1939 George S. Kaufman and Moss Hart. Copyright renewal 1966 Catherine Carlisle Hart and Anne Kaufman Schneider. All rights reserved.

Charles Scribner's Sons: Henry Van Dyke, "America for Me" and "Mare Liberum" from *The Poems of Henry Van Dyke*. Copyright 1911 Charles Scribner's Sons; copyright renewed 1939 Tertius Van Dyke. Struthers Burt, "The Full-Fledged American" from *Escape from America*. Copyright 1936 Charles Scribner's Sons; copyright renewed © 1964 Struthers Burt. Reprinted with the permission of Charles Scribner's Sons.

Viking Penguin Inc. and Wm. Heinemann Ltd.: A selection from *Travels with Charley* by John Steinbeck. Copyright © 1961, 1962 by The Curtis Publishing Co., Inc. Copyright © 1962 by John Steinbeck. Reprinted by permission of Viking Penguin Inc. and Wm. Heinemann Ltd.

A. P. Watt Ltd: An extract from *Pilgrim's Way* by John Buchan entitled "My America." By permission of The Rt. Hon. the Lord Tweedsmuir, CBE.

Yale University Press: A selection from *In the Green Mountain Country* by Clarence Day.